T0307845

In the Shade of
the Shady Tree

Also by John Kinsella

in the shade
of the
shady tree

STORIES OF WHEATBELT AUSTRALIA

John Kinsella

Swallow Press / Ohio University Press
Athens

Swallow Press / Ohio University Press, Athens, Ohio 45701
www.ohioswallow.com

Printed in the United States of America
Swallow Press / Ohio University Press books are printed on acid-free
paper ⊗ ™

20 19 18 17 16 15 14 13 12   5 4 3 2 1

Library of Congress Cataloging-in-Publication Data
Kinsella, John, 1963–
 In the shade of the shady tree : stories of wheatbelt Australia / John
Kinsella.
    p. cm.
 ISBN 978-0-8040-1137-2 (hc : acid-free paper)
 1. Western Australia—Fiction. I. Title.
 PR9619.3.K55I5 2012
 823'.914—dc22

                        2011043285

for Tracy, as always

A journey through the West
Australian wheatbelt and adjacent
southern areas: from north to south.

The author wishes to acknowledge
the traditional owners and
custodians of the land he writes: the
Yamatji and Nyungar peoples.

contents

preface

Last night a storm hit this drought-ravaged place without warning. It was a brutal assault. We kept our roof, but neighbors lost theirs. There are a number of large York gums down—snapped off low on their trunks. Inside the trunks, the soil welded by excreta and saliva of termites crumbles out. So many of the trees here are hollowed by termites. Echidnas scrape at the base of the trees for termites—we often see their telltale diggings, but rarely the nocturnal echidnas themselves.

We received thirty-two millimeters of rain last night, the most in a single downfall for five years. It's a reprieve for a lot of the life on this block and the surrounding area—drought has killed many trees, and the effect on wildlife has become evident. It has been diminishing, not only from lack of water, but from increasing pressure of human occupation.

On lands that are traditionally Ballardong Nyungar, clearing and poisoning and other abuses of place have taken their toll, and continue to do so. Just over the hill begin the vast wheat and sheep farms of the Victoria Plains district, part of the Western Australian wheatbelt. Devastation caused by this monocultural farming is seen in ever-increasing land salinity, and in changing local weather patterns, due not only to larger global processes but also to localized land-clearing.

I first entered the wheatbelt when I was a few weeks old. My uncle and aunt's farm, Wheatlands, was a beacon of my childhood. As I grew up, I spent many weekends and holidays at Wheatlands. The grain silos, heart of the many towns that dot the wheatbelt's hundred and fifty thousand square kilometers, are fed by farms like Wheatlands, often handed down through generations. Nowadays, they are breaking up as eldest sons no longer inherit the lot. Divided up between the children, the farms are often sold on to large companies: corporate agriculture.

The history of the wheatbelt is multicultural, though the divisions of spoils are lopsided. Anglo-Celtic colonizers ("settler"-migrants) dispossessed the indigenous peoples in the nineteenth century and exacted their labor. Colonists later relied on convicts (petitioning for their presence in the colony!), then migrants who came with the 1890s gold rush, and still later the great migrations prompted by conflict in twentieth-century Europe: Italians, Yugoslavs, Greeks, Poles, and many others were paid a pittance to clear the bush for grain growing. Some of these people eventually established their own farms and their own dynasties. Others failed. For every success in the wheatbelt there is a failure. It is harsh in many ways.

My poetics and sensibilities formed not only in the paddocks and remnant bushland, but also on the vast salt scalds where very little grew or even lived. But there was life there if you looked; and I *did* look. Though they were the result of European overfarming, and truly a blight on the land, I discovered, in the gullies and scalds of "the salt," mysteries, wonders and beauties that have fascinated me all my life. Complex formations of salt crystals, the "puff and bubble" of salt tissue over mud, the harsh reflector beds of white in summers that reach the high 40s centigrade. My entire poetic output has been grounded in the contradictions of the terror and beauty of salinity.

Yet it is not only poetry I have written through my life: there are also stories. The poetry has been about place in a very empirical way, concerned with damage and its implications. But in my stories I am more concerned with glimpses of the people who live in the wheatbelt. Whether I approve of their activities or not is irrelevant. What is at issue is how they interact with the place, and how they make that place what it is. I am interested in the weirdness that comes from the ordinary, the extraordinary from the matter-of-fact. The behavior of people seems more odd to me than, say, supernatural belief. I ask how secrecy is part of everyone's lives, and how disturbance goes hand-in-hand with the predictable. A good deed can mask ill intent; a bad deed can result from well-meaning acts. There are rarely neat resolutions, and other than death, few absolute conclusions. Even death leaves loose threads, many loose threads.

Underlying all these glimpses is the knowledge and acknowledgment that I am writing a land stolen from indigenous people; that in truth it is still their land, if it's anyone's. I have never believed in property per se, nor in "ownership." I see my role in this place as one of "carer," one who has a responsibility to observe, discuss, and even protect.

But these stories aim to do something else: they are a jigsaw puzzle that offers the reader, I hope, a way of seeing how small fragments of the place work, or don't work. Some have fable-like morals, others are fantastical, but many are just "insights" into an aspect of being here. I am interested in the glimpse into character, and how that character is affected by "place." No one's entire story can really be told. Yet many stories or glimpses added together, collated on a journey, might give us a broader picture of the so-called human condition.

In the vein of one of my favorite Australian story writers, Henry Lawson, I really see them as yarns: stories told for the moment, out of experience more than "art." But they are informed by an artfulness, if not an art. One of my favorite volumes of American stories is Sherwood Anderson's *Winesburg, Ohio*, which most would know is artifice on the level of story but "truthful" in the insights it gives into living in a small town somewhere in Midwest America, if not in the eponymous town itself. I lived in Ohio with my family for a number of years. Our son was born there. I see it as a home. We went looking at the real Winesburg knowing it wasn't the Winesburg constructed by

Anderson. And that was okay—it interested us to see how the stories had affected the town, and of course, they had.

When we write place, we necessarily contribute to a view of what that place is—even such a vast place as the Western Australian wheatbelt with its many, many towns, varying in size from the seven thousand population of a regional center like Northam to the handful of residents in places like Jennacubbine. Our contribution to the view of the place is always disproportionate, even if only read by a single reader. Because the life of that place is only ever a glimpse, is selective, and often largely a construct. And that's true of this book as well. The stories herein follow a roadmap from the northernmost point of the wheatbelt, up near Northampton, down to the Great Southern, where the wheatbelt becomes something else. Each town passed through is given a tale that might or might not capture something "real" about that town or its district.

What I hope the book captures is something about people, and the way people make lives of place and alter that place in doing so. What happens in one story in one town or district might just as easily happen three hundred kilometers away in another part of the wheatbelt. But the stories did come out of those places, so immediately a sense of belonging or maybe alienation locates itself quite specifically on the compass. I find these apparent contradictions fascinating.

I have lived with my family on and off in the wheatbelt for many years. I am quite reclusive, but when I emerge I look and listen closely. I am part of the district, especially around York, where I have lifelong family connections and lived for many years; Northam, the main center of the same region; and the hills north of Toodyay, which we now call "home." Each of these locales has had disasters and incidents that have brought communities close together and also divided them. Then there are those figures who always remain outside any community. They also interest me. As does how "isolated" farming places (I have always been interested in the particulars of farming, whether I agree with aspects of them or not) connect or distance themselves from the world at large. The prejudices, bigotries, and scepticisms need to be read and "glimpsed," as much as the affirmations.

I went to high school in the midwest seaside town of Geraldton (now a small city of thirty-two thousand), about 420 kilometers north of the state capital, Perth. Geraldton is a fishing, farming, and mining town. The huge wheat farms that edge the coast are carved out of "sandplain" and are worked using vast amounts of superphosphate and chemical sprays. As a kid, I spent time with my father on a thirty-thousand-acre farm near Mullewa, east of Geraldton. There were tractors with wheels twice my height (machinery at once disturbs and fascinates me). I was traumatized by the clear evidence that the Yamatji people of the region were cut off from their traditional lands, and by the suffering this brought. I had long been familiar with gun culture and saw on a large scale what hunting was all about. By the time I was in my very early twenties, I had become a dedicated vegan. I had the experience to make a clear-cut choice. I did plenty of damage to birds, fish, and animals as a child and a teenager.

When I was twenty, I went away to Mingenew in the northern wheatbelt to work on the wheatbins. Enormous receiving silos. I was a protein sampler. I used the money earned to travel through Europe. I went back the next season and came into conflict with an ex–South African mercenary who was driving a grain truck and held extreme racist views. I resisted and was punished. I witnessed bigoted and aggressive behaviors during that stint that I hope never to witness again. This is always in the back of my mind. But so is positive experience, such as ploughing under the stars on Wheatlands farm, or looking after the farm over summer months—a twenty-one-year-old with responsibility for a large farm is something else. Or again, planting avocado trees with my uncle as he tried to diversify out of monocultural farming, or helping plant trees (they planted tens of thousands) in saline areas to try to reclaim damaged land.

All of these aspects are part of the wheatbelt for me. Giant "food bowl" that it is, its "feeding the world," as they like to say, has come at a great cost to indigenous people and to the land itself. It has also come at a cost, ironically, to those who colonized, cleared, farmed, and lived there. The suicide rate, especially among males, is phenomenally high, and the sad spectacle of a land dying through salinity and drought goes hand-in-hand with more damage and more misunderstanding of denying the consequences.

In the end, it's a place of people: their successes and failures, of materiality and spirit. Though the wheatbelt is bound together by the central activity of grain farming, it ranges in geography from coastal plains to semi-arid marginal land, on the edge of the outback, producing very low yields, through to much richer lands (though the soils are still impoverished, there are higher rainfalls) in places such as the Avon Valley, with its ancient river course formed by the Wagyl spirit outside time, and holding the ancient eroded Dyott Range.

To tell more of the place, maybe it's best just to describe a few towns from the wheatbelt. Following are some of the towns with which I am very familiar, and which in many ways form reference points in my own journey. These are not historical renderings, but impressions formed from living in the regions. In some ways, maybe they are stories in themselves.

York

Earliest inland settlement in Western Australia, founded in 1829. The governor had a residence there, and the police searched for escaped convicts and suppressed the indigenous inhabitants from its police station. The old court building is a tourist site now. Homeland of the Ballardong Nyungar people. I have been in and out of York since I was born—my uncle's farm, "Wheatlands," was twenty kilometers northeast. For many years we lived about five kilometers north of town. My mother still lives there. Some call it the "gateway to the wheatbelt."

As rainfalls have dropped and drought has gripped, an "historic" town such as York has begun to rely increasingly on weekend visits from the city of Perth, a hundred kilometers southwest. York's early stone buildings, its "colonial history," and the area's deeply spiritual significance to the Nyungar people make it a standout in the state.

The town, located on the Avon River, is remarkably beautiful, though the surrounding land has been much damaged by attempts to "train" the river to prevent flooding—that is, dredging it so waterholes, which would once have survived the brutal summers, no longer existed—and devastating salinity caused by overclearing of surrounding lands, as well as clearing of riparian vegetation. In fact, it's one of the few spots where water stays in the river all year round, even in drought.

Cradled between the small mountain of Walwalinj, or Mount Bakewell as named by explorer Ensign Dale, and Wongborel, known to the settlers as Mount Brown, York is at the crossroads of the Avon Valley. A fiercely independent-minded town, it is home to the deeply religious as well as to the heretical and nonbelieving. Christianity in many denominations is prevalent, and if it isn't "Bible-fearing," as some of the more inland wheatbelt towns are, the manners of belief there are always in the background. Anglican gentility informs much of the cultural endeavor of the town, whether it's an arts festival or baroque music in Holy Trinity, across the swing bridge over the Avon River. But there's a Catholic church that looks like a small cathedral, and there are halls and meetinghouses of other churches.

Developers eye York with glee; the friction is intense between those who would make a buck and leave and those who see York as a chosen lifestyle place. Bounded on one side by wandoo bushland and by York gum/jam tree woodlands on another, the place suffers more clearing and damage each year. It is conservative, but with a sprinkling of radicals who are generally tolerated because York prides itself on being a cultural place. That's European-derived culture. But it's also a center of Nyungar culture, where the strength lies. There is racism and division in the town, but possibly less so than elsewhere.

One of the current greats of Australian Rules football comes from York, and white and black are intensely proud of him. But the town is still subtly controlled by the power of land ownership. The big voices are the big farmers. I wrote a number of these stories in the historic York Post Office building, designed by Temple-Poole in the second half of the nineteenth century, where I had an office within the two-foot-thick stone walls. On the single main street running south to north, I looked out over the day-to-day activities of the town. An incident outside the bottle shop, dogs barking on the back of utes, as Australians call pickups.

Northam

Main town of the central wheatbelt and Avon Valley. A regional center of some seven thousand people, providing the only senior high school for vast distances. It services the broader farming community of the region. The railway here has been important over the years, and one of the largest inland grain-receival points sits on the outskirts of town. The wide paddocks that spread throughout the region carry crops of wheat, barley, oats, canola, and other seeds/grains. Wheat is the mainstay. It is railed and trucked from the bins to the ports (primarily Fremantle/Kwinana) for export. An historic and still functioning flour mill sits on the river at the southeastern end of town. Shearing is also a major industry, with shearing teams buying their gear, drinking, and often living there when not out working the sheds.

Northam has a regional hospital, the main regional courts, and a large police station. It is a violent town, with a high crime rate and often literally blood on the streets, especially outside the hotels. It used to have a small cinema complex, but that closed down because of late-night violence. It has an active and high-quality amateur dramatic company that uses a theater based in an old church building—farce and comedy are their mainstay, which draws locals. The high school puts on an annual play there—our daughter featured in the production of *A Midsummer Night's Dream*. There is also a regional art gallery. There are four large old-style drinking hotels, and a lengthy main street with shops, plus a small arcade.

Sports are a big part of the town's life, dominated by Australian Rules football, netball, and cricket. This is true of most wheatbelt towns, but there is much more infrastructure in Northam. Our daughter used to bus a seventy-kilometer round trip to school. An historic town, with the legendary, introduced white swans that have been a feature of European colonization here for over a hundred years. It is the starting point of the famed (and environmentally destructive) Avon Descent, the longest whitewater boat race in the southern hemisphere; that's in years when there's any water to race along.

After the Second World War, the town housed many European migrants. Their tales of hardship adjusting to the heat and flies and Spartan conditions are told in a commemorative display at the tourist center. Ironically, given this, Northam has a racist history. Many of the Ballardong Nyungar families of the region were broken up, and the place is notorious for the removal from their Nyungar families of children who were considered to have "white blood." These children were part of the horrendous reality of the Stolen Generations, the damage of which resounds to this day. Many of the children ended up at the Moore River Settlement, several days' walk away.

Recently, Northam's racism and bigotry have run out of control with the announcement of a refugee holding center, for Afghan males, to be established at the old army base. You cannot walk the streets without being confronted by signs screaming "Parasites," or demonstrations with people wearing T-shirts that declare, "Send back their boats" or "Bomb their boats." There *is* a more liberal side to the town (though small in number), who call for humanity and respect for all peoples.

But Northam is a divided town; its indigenous inhabitants experience racism on a daily basis. I was one of those who refused to shop at a major supermarket until charges were dropped against one Nyungar boy (and he was clearly labeled "black" as a pejorative in the media) who was threatened with serious theft charges for possessing an unpaid-for chocolate frog (given to him by a cousin).

On the positive side, there is a firm sense of identity in the black community, with two of the town's primary schools having 40 percent or more indigenous pupils and significant cultural programmes. The Wheatbelt Aboriginal Corporation is also based there, and there are strong bonds across the various communities outside the racist elements.

Northam is a strongly Christian town (Irish Catholics have been an historically dominant group, along with Anglicans; Baptists and other Protestant denominations now have a strong presence), with deeply conservative views on race, sexuality, and ethnicity. It is also the arts center of the region. The banks and government offices are there, and people from a hundred kilometers or more away do their big shopping and essential business there.

Toodyay

Another early inland town, originally called Newcastle, and at first built on a flood area of the Avon River, despite warnings from Nyungar people that the settlers would be washed out in winter. The town was moved, and the name later changed to avoid clashing with one of the same name in the then colony of New South Wales.

"Toodyay" is derived from a Ballardong Nyungar word meaning "place of plenty." The area around Toodyay remains rich in native bush and wildlife. There are wandoo, marri, and jarrah woodlands, and York and jam tree environments, such as on our own place. We live about fifteen kilometers north of the town, on a bush block that sees many kangaroos pass by on any given day; that has bobtails and western black monitors, mulga snakes and gwarders, and a wide range of birds, including twenty-eight parrots, red-capped robins, eagles, and tawny frogmouths. There's an echidna on the block—I see its scratchings daily but have yet to come across it. Our place is strewn with granite and "Toodyay stone," and there are large granite boulders at the top of the block. The soils around the shire vary from infertile sand to a richer red loam (still low in nutrients).

It's a tough area—shearers (my brother, further north, is a shearer), farm laborers, bikers, fly-in fly-out miners (who fly north for two weeks on at the interior mines, and back for two weeks off), hobby farms and large spreads mixed together. Jack Daniels and beer are the drinks of choice, and the rock band AC/DC rules. Every year there is a jazz festival in the main street of town, and also the Moondyne Festival, named after a bushranger and escape artist who hid in the hills around the town for many years. Toodyay residents often see themselves as outlaws, and indeed some are. It's a place of bushy beards and raven-haired women with tats. Alternative lifestylers (Orange People, Wiccans, hermits) live alongside horse breeders, middle-class wine imbibers, and weekend farmers traveling up from the city.

Toodyay is at the edge of the Darling Range, and the Avon River cuts through a range of smaller valleys and hills. It is considered picturesque and is much visited, but in many ways it is a hard-living and violent town. Ferociously hot during summer, it is a high fire-risk area because of the large amount of bush still nestled among the hills. Late in 2009, thousands of acres were devastated by fire, with the loss of thirty-nine houses, many sheds, and many animals. There were no human deaths, though a life was lost in a bushfire here two years before.

Mullewa

Another old inland town, but in the Murchison area six or more hours' drive north of the capital, Perth. Intensely hot and dry. Home of the Yamatji people, also an area rich in spiritual significance. A place of intense racism on the part of the whites living there. The town is deeply divided and violence is frequent within and between communities.

Mullewa is surrounded by, and services, massive farms. During the seventies my father managed a thirty-thousand-acre spread there, owned by a notorious Perth (and international) millionaire. It is a gun culture out there. In this relatively low rainfall area, the huge sandplain farms rely on large acreages to yield enough to make farming profitable. It's also a large sheep running area. My brother shears there year-in year-out, being based in the region. He and I went to high school in the regional center, Geraldton, positioned on the coast and about seventy kilometers from Mullewa.

When the paddocks aren't sand, they are a red dirt almost the color of blood. The vegetation is low and scrubby, with patches of taller trees along the waterways and places where more moisture accumulates. In spring the entire region, at least the uncleared bits and along roadsides, erupts with wildflowers. Tourists drive through at that time of the year, but don't stay.

The town is still strongly Catholic, and not too far away is Devil's Creek. Names mean so much, and hide so much. The town has some superb architecture by the Catholic missionary architect Monsignor Hawes, whose churches and associated buildings can be found throughout the northern wheatbelt.

It could be argued that the nonindigenous "side" of the town and the region still perceive themselves as pioneers in many ways. As a kid I got trapped here in a silo with my brother, and met hard, gnarled farm workers who told me about booze, and from whom I learnt that women could piss standing up. Guns were never far away; it was the home of many roo-shooters. I started to understand what real horror was. I used to stare into the blank centers of starflowers and wonder. I also used to trap parrots that bit through my fingers.

acknowledgments

ABC Radio National, *The Advertiser, The Age, Agni, Antipodes, Best Australian Stories 2006* (edited by Robert Drewe), *Best Australian Stories 2007* (edited by Robert Drewe), *Best Australian Stories 2010* (edited by Kate Kennedy), *Crazyhorse, Families: Modern Australian Short Stories* (volume 6, edited by Barry Oakley), *Griffith Review, Island, Kenyon Review, The Literary Review, Meanjin, The Reader, Southerly, StoryQuarterly*. Also to the Literature Board of the Australia Council for a two-year New Work grant to assist in the writing of these stories, and special acknowledgment to the University of Western Australia for a Professorial Research Fellowship and its ongoing support. Thanks to my editor at Ohio University Press, Gillian Berchowitz, for her hard work, sharp insights, and good advice.

rain

★Mullewa

Ben gets on the phone immediately and rings his brother, who farms two hours' drive away. It's raining! he yells. Really raining. It's raining! What's it like at your place? Nothing here, replies his brother in a subdued tone. Ben then rings his neighbor, whose three thousand acres share a boundary with his three thousand acres. How's it comin' down at your place? he asks. It's not, replies the neighbor . . . I can see the black clouds in the distance, about over your place, I reckon, but nothing here at my house yet. Not even sure that it will rain here . . . not much of a breeze, but what there is, is blowin' away from my place.

Ben hangs up and rings his neighbor on the other side, whose property doesn't actually join his property—there is a large granite nature reserve between them—but is the next on down the road. Not a drop, mate, and it doesn't look like it's coming our way. And I'm starin' at the wall barometer, and nothin's changed. Same as yesterday, the day before, last month. There's bitterness on the other end of the phone, and Ben doesn't know what to say, so he just hangs up and walks back to the window to watch the rain bucket down.

It continues to rain. It rains all day and through the night into the next morning. And into the afternoon. He rings around again. Same story. We're not even seeing any runoff, mate, your place is like a sink, all flows into the middle and then down the creeks into the river. By the time it hits that dry riverbed it sinks into the sand. You're the only bloke gettin' weather, and the runoff stops at your boundaries!

What starts as a joy, a reason for celebration, becomes disturbing. Ben has stayed inside during the rain, having been a bit crook of late. But he is feeling better, and decides he'll go and check over his property. He kits up in his wet-weather gear and heads out through the back door to make his way over to the machinery shed where the ute is parked. He checks the rain gauge. An unbelievable fifty points! Then it dawns on him that the rain has suddenly stopped—that it stopped the moment he stepped out into the open. A few drops hit his hands and then it stopped. He looks up at the sky and it starts to clear. It swirls and convulses and the sun breaks through the clouds. Then he notices that where the rain has touched his skin the skin burns slightly, guiltily.

Driving along the fence line of paddock after paddock, he finds it's the same story everywhere. A strong green carpet of growth has appeared on his side of the divide. He will start seeding immediately. There's been no *serious* thought of it for the last couple of years. He's put crops in, like everyone else, but other than some short, light falls there's been nothing. His immediate neighbors have culled their sheep flocks for want of feed. Distant neighbors have auctioned off plant to meet bills. Ben has hung in there, bringing feed in from his brother's place, which has managed to yield enough hay for that purpose—enough to feed his own animals and to sell to friends to keep theirs alive—but that's it. He's held on to all his machinery.

Ben sees a measure of how much it has rained when he arrives at the salty ground in the dead center of the property. It is, indeed, a sink, with the two creeks that branch out of its heart winding their way down through the rubbish dumped as "landfill" there over the years, like a rush of blood through clogged arteries—an arteriosclerosis of the farm. Rolls of fencing wire, old spray drums, wood, even a seized truck motor. It doesn't look healthy, Ben whispers to himself, so quietly he can hardly hear it.

Arriving back at the house paddock, he starts planning the seeding. He has enough seed grain, and the machinery is all in good working order. He has had nothing much to do other than mess around with it and keep it working. He will lightly work the soil then seed and fertilize. He heads back up to the house.

But the *moment* he steps inside, he hears the rain on the roof again. It spooks him, because he glanced up at the sky before he stepped onto the verandah, and it had pretty well entirely cleared. Barely a cloud.

Now he stares out of the window at the black swollen skies and the hard driving rain. Harder than during the days before. A deluge. He feels giddy. He sees the farm under water. He sees the green carpet become the algal floor of a fetid ocean. He sees the corpses of a thousand sheep marooned on the granite outcrop, with the ocean of his farm lapping at their hooves. He collapses into a chair and cries. He hasn't cried since he was a small child. His mother forbade him to cry because his father found it embarrassing and she never liked to see her husband, whom she loved so much, upset. Your father is such a good provider, she'd say again and again, a mantra. It's unbecoming to cry, son. Ben's tears rain down over the slightly greasy tablecloth, and he can't hold them back. A deluge.

I must stop, he yells, to no one but himself. He pauses. Then he cries: It! It It! I must stop *it*! The house resounds with the words, the gravel out of his throat. The lampshade vibrates overhead, disturbed. The lampshade he's done so many farm accounts under; that he did his school homework under while his mother prepared the dinner in the kitchen before telling him to set the table because *father* was due in from the paddocks . . . I must stop *it!*

Ben tears his clothes off piece by piece. He can hear the rain driving into the tin roof so hard he sees nails. He sees fencing wire stretched so taut it snaps. He hears a wheel-nut shear from being overtightened and a bullwhip being cracked at the show. Everything taut and tense finally reaches its point of no return. He prays for the rain to cut through the roof, through the ceiling insulation, through the ceiling itself, to cut up his now-bare body. He raises his arms to the deluge and speaks as he imagines a great biblical figure would have spoken when confronted by the harshness of God's judgment, Why have you chosen me, why have you left me in the wilderness so long only to reward me when it is too late? He demands to know. He pleads.

Naked, he runs through the back door and out into the rain. He feels the rain strike his body and burn away the dry, flaky outer layer of skin. A snake shedding its skin. A moulting.

And then the rain stops.

Ben looks around. He hears the parrots laughing in the York gums. He covers his burning nakedness with his hands and slinks back into the house. The rain doesn't start again. Nothing. He dresses and goes to bed without eating, sleeps all night and through the next day. When he wakes, there is *no rain* on the roof. He rings his brother. Been no rain here, Ben, says his brother in the same limp voice. He rings his two neighbors. No rain, mate. No rain, mate. They ask how it's going out at his place—must be good with all that rain he's had. Ben can taste their bitterness. Most of it just rolled off the surface into the creeks—made it look like more than there really was, he says. Only a few points in the gauge for a couple of days, in the end. Not enough to start seeding, I'm afraid.

Ben wants to reassure them all. He keeps talking, Well, just enough rain, I guess . . . but it's not worth wasting my seed grain when there's no chance of any weather down the track. The long-range forecast is for dry days and cold nights. Thought my ship had come in, but it hadn't. You can't bet your life's savings on such long odds . . . Hah, nah, didn't amount to much. Not so strange after all . . . really.

He wanted to stop reassuring them—his brother, his neighbors, himself—but his skin still tingled with the burning of the rain.

purchase

★ Northampton

They had their hearts set on purchasing a piece
of land up north, but not too far north. Coastal—or as near
coastal as they might afford. Close to a town for supplies, but
not *too* close to a town: they wanted privacy and a sense of
having "got away" from it all. This wasn't really a "sea change"
(as the trendies and media would have it)—going down to the
city had been that, for them. They were country people who'd
retired from the farm early and given the city a go. Now they
wanted out. But not a place on a large scale. A small property
of, say, thirty acres. Grow a few olives, keep a few sheep for
hobby shearing, nothing more.

A suitable block came up not long after their search began.
They visited a small town close to the Batavia Coast and had
a chat with the local real estate agent. There was nothing up
in the sales window, but she had her ear to the ground, as real
estate agents do, and knew of a property about to go on the
market. The owners had only had it for a year, so it was good
luck they were selling—land in the region was at a premium

6

and much sought after. There was a waiting list but, recognizing like minds—she was a farmer's daughter—and the prospect of cash on the button, she "juggled" her list.

The boy watched his dad's car emerge out of the setting sun and speed down the gravel driveway, the back end dropping out in clouds of dust, then pulled back into line. Perched on his trail bike on the hill, he glanced across at the people walking the neighboring property with the real estate agent. He revved the engine and dropped the clutch, spinning the back wheel and kicking dirt and stones out towards the newcomers. They were too far away to be hit by the debris, but not too far to sense some kind of aggression. They stared at the boy zigzagging over the crest of the hill—that bare property next door . . . not a tree on it.

For a moment, the couple basked in the neat mixture of clear space and white gums they were buying. And they had (for in their minds it was already theirs) a small hill as well—looked like an old mine on the far side, to the east, but it'd been filled in or blasted shut. The estate agent said she didn't know much about it, but could guarantee it was entirely sealed and there was no risk of sheep wandering in and being lost. As an ex-farmer, the man—or Darl, as his wife called him—took a close look, and agreed. *Perfectly safe!* At the access road end of the property—to the west—there was a creek, dry midsummer. Plenty of water too: a well had been sunk and there was a dam in the western corner which would catch the entire flow off their hill, and off their neighbor's. The couple was going to sign off on the deal that evening—one last wander around and chat with the agent.

The boy's dad had only had a few drinks after work, and was in a sardonic yet almost pleasant mood. The boy had

to tell him now. If he left it till later, his dad would go spare.
It was the boy's job to keep a lookout. And then, if Dad was
really pissed when he discovered for himself—because he
would, because all the blokes at the pub were his dad's spies
and they'd know quick as lightning—he'd give him a good
kicking for holding back the info.

Dad, I saw that bitch real-estate agent with some new people. The
boy steadily ripped open a Coke and kept his eyes to himself.
The fizz of the can would be the prelude to . . . *Jeez! What now?!
Can't get any privacy round this fucking place. Get rid of one lot and
another rolls in. Bitch! Fucking bitch! I've got her number . . . give it
time, give it time.* His dad stopped there and the boy knew the
silence meant his dad *did* have a plan for the real estate agent.
She'd keep. And when his dad fixed things, he really fixed
things. In the meantime, he sensed his dad switch attention to
the problem immediately at hand.

Taking a bottle of spirits from the cupboard, the bearded
miner called the boy to get his lazy carcass into the kitchen and
cook him a steak. That was the night Dad was supposed to eat
at the pub before getting home. The boy looked after himself
on these nights—he was good at that. Even though he only had
his dad, his mum had gone a long time back, he liked it out on
the block alone. He was never scared . . . only when his dad got
back from the pub. The boy started to walk towards his room.
Hey, where do you think you're going? Cook your dad a steak!

To get their new place started, the couple went south to
Batavia and picked up an old donga from a construction
company. It was to be delivered in a few weeks—enough time to
clear a pad for it and sort out the details of their move from the
city. The plan was to live in the donga for as long as it took to
get their new house established. They'd always wanted to build.

Though Batavia was much further away than the small
town where the real estate agent plied her trade, they stayed

in a motel down there because it was easier to get things done.
They arranged for workers to go up and build the pad—being
on site to ensure it went in the right place, of course. Choosing
to work with an architect to design the plans themselves, they
shopped around builders for the best product. It was an exciting
time, though—somewhat ironically—one during which they
barely had a chance to be at the new place!

The couple was out there to see the donga set to rest. And
it was then they met the boy on the trail bike . . . heard his dad
yelling in the distance. A stream of abuse they were unable
to interpret. They thought the dad drunk and best avoided.
Nonetheless, it was an exquisite day, and it reminded them of
their best times on the farm. After the harvest check was in, and
they didn't have to worry about money for a while. That kind
of feeling. And the pressures of the city were gone. Down there,
drunks were never far away either—it was no big deal.

But what the boy had to say bothered them a little. Darl
more than his wife. *Pet,* he said to her, *these neighbors aren't all
there. They're a few planks short of a jetty.* He enjoyed sayings like
that. He always smiled after using them, even when concerned.
To be honest, Darl thought it bullshit and was suspicious of the
kid anyway. Looked like a dope smoker. You get them on small
properties—Darl hadn't come down in the last shower. But given
the place next door didn't have a bit of green on it, he reasoned
the boy wasn't growing it there, and that was all he cared about.

The boy was nervous, even frantic around his father. *So I
told them like you said, Dad. I told them it was an old lead mine and
that the tailings are all over the block. That the place is poison. That
there's lead in the well water. Just like I told the other people.*

—And what happened? his dad growled. *I think it worked.
The old girl looked scared and the bloke with a pole up his arse stared at*

*me without saying anything. Their names are Pet and Darl. I've heard
them call each other that.*

The boy's dad laughed and then repeated to himself, *Pet and
Darl . . . Pet and Darl . . . bloody dickheads.*

Then, dead quiet. The boy watched his father, trying hard not
to tap his foot or do anything else that'd set the burly miner off.

Bastards, the drunken miner muttered. *Bastards . . . sticking
that eyesore there without so much as a by-your-leave. Who do they
think they are? Squatters? The landed fucking gentry?* He then started
yelling again, punching a fist into a hand: *No neighbors! No
neighbors! No neighbors!* The corellas, scratching at the dirt and
eyeing the neighbor's spread, squawked en masse and plumed
into the air, settling on the other side of the fence.

Pet rang the real estate agent just to check about the
abandoned "lead mine." The voice hesitated only slightly on the
other end: *Don't worry about it, the kid's got a mental problem . . . He's
known in town for making up stories. Always being suspended from school.
My daughter knows him . . . says he's weird. Don't worry, though. I think
he's harmless.* Pet could tell the agent was clutching at straws.

The prospect of coexistence—even distantly—with a
drunkard and a weird kid distracted them from the lead
business. Darl did say, though, *I should probably get the place tested.*
And Pet carried out a quick Internet search at a Batavia café,
and found that there were in fact lead mines throughout the
area, and that lead had been detected in local well water. Dogs
had died from it. She insisted. He said, *Well, we haven't got any
dogs and we haven't got any small children . . .* She could hear that
he was becoming a farmer again.

But Pet wouldn't let it go. She couldn't. And as they stood
in their donga looking out at a blood-red sunset, the drunk
next door screaming across the distance, in ragged bursts
that punctuated lulls in the fresh sea-breeze: *No neighbors! No
neighbors! No neighbors!* she caught Darl's eye twitching—a

sign that he was reaching the end of his tolerance. He wasn't a violent man, but still he had a temper. He'd give that drunken neighbor a run for his money, then there'd be real trouble. Pet felt it in her waters. *Well, the town has been drinking the water for a hundred years, so I think we'll survive,* Darl said suddenly, and calmly. As if that was that, and there'd be no more talk about the matter. Gradually they both decided they couldn't care less about the lead. Even if it were true, they'd live there. They had once been farmers. Back then, they had saturated their paddocks and animals in poison every year. *What was the difference? Real estate agents will say anything.* They remained proud of their purchase.

The donga had been there for a few weeks and workers were already laying the house-pad. The boy's father was mumbling something about the next phase of the operation. The night before, he'd fired rifle shots into the air and played the stereo extra loud.

Funny thing was, the boy had watched the donga being set in place with a dull excitement—almost creeping skin—as the crane hoisted the donga from the semi-trailer. Overwidth, overlength. The cops were there—a car out front, a car behind the load. That'd cost them. And he'd watched in amazement as the ground was leveled for the pad. The boy liked how *precise* it all was. The old couple—Pet and Darl . . . he drawled their names sarcastically, mimicking his father—weren't there much, but when they were he rode along the fence line on his motorbike, revving the shit out of the engine as per his dad's instruction. Darl would watch him doing this for an age, and the boy thought he saw the old bloke shaking as if he were really angry once, but it might have been the easterly that had whipped in, hot and burning though it was only spring.

When the truck and workers and new owners were gone, the boy rode his trail bike up to a tear in the fence and wormed the bike through. He rode over to the mine, got off, and threw tailings at the crumpled and suffocated entry. Phase two of his dad's plan to cleanse the district of invaders. Then he mounted up and raced down to the creek. He leant his head so far back he nearly fell off his bike—he was looking up at the sun through white gum leaves, the oil of the trees headier than dope. His dad was a smart man.

It was an "earthquake-proofed" house. A steel frame with single brick and plasterboard walls, built on a sand pad. The boy was fascinated. He rode over and asked the builders about it. Dad was at work and he was wagging school, so it would be okay. He was bored. *Earthquake-proof, eh? We haven't had an earthquake here, I don't think,* he said to them. A gnarled and bearded builder with tobacco stains around his mouth and moustache said: *Well, some people like to be prepared, matey.* The builder asked the boy to pass him his beer, cool in its foam holder. *Yep, nothing like working in the bush,* he said, *no problem drinking on the job.* He hacked and spat as he laughed.

The builder paused as he set a string for a new line of bricks, and said to the boy, who was rocking his bike back and forth so its wheels bit into the dirt, *So you've been a bit of a bastard to my employers?* The boy looked away and said: *My dad doesn't like neighbors.*

Yeah, well, your dad's being an arsehole. The boy shot a look back at the builder and sized up the opposition: the guy was built like a brick shithouse. Ten axe handles across. Sunburnt and milky-eyed with drink. But still sharp. The boy wanted to say something back, but hit the kick-start with his boot and throttled up, spewing sand all over the place as he raced back to the hole in the fence.

The boy stared at his dad spread-eagled on the couch, watching television. *What are you staring at, you little bastard,* his father half-asked him.

—Nothing. They're putting the roof on the place next door. *Who gives a damn,* his dad muttered, taking the boy by surprise. Dad looked strange. It worried the boy.

Darl and Pet were living in the donga, waiting for their house to be completed. It wouldn't be long now. The summer had set in, and it was getting pretty hot even through the nights—they craved the ducted air-conditioning they'd had installed in their dream home. The power was through, and they'd made the massive outlay to have scheme water put on. Darl said, *It's not because of this bull about the quality of groundwater around here, just that it's more reliable.* It was late, and in the cramped space they were watching television, doing dishes and talking over the plans when there was a knock at the door. The husband called out, *Who's there?*

—It's me, from next door . . .

The couple looked at each other. *Don't open it,* Pet said. Darl looked at her for slightly too long, then shook his head and went to open it. The boy was standing on the step shaking. His hair was slicked to his forehead with sweat. *What's happened?* asked Darl. Pet was behind her husband's shoulder now, and seeing the boy, pushed her way through and placed her hand on his arm. *What's wrong, son? What's happened?*

—It's my dad. He's sick. I mean he's really sick. I think he needs a doctor and the phone isn't working. I mean, Dad broke the phone when he got in from work.

Darl didn't mind paying the extra for scheme water to be piped out to the place. Cost thousands, but peace of mind is peace of mind. Probably nothing wrong, but why go through the worry? The real estate agent's sister—a nurse at the hospital—said tests showed there was nothing wrong with the groundwater. That's what the real estate agent reckoned. But what the hell. And when Darl suggested to the boy's dad he connect his place to the scheme for a few thousand, the ex-drunk surprisingly said yes. *I can taste the bloody water now,* he mumbled—*when we ran out of rainwater, the well water tasted pretty bad, didn't it, boy?*

—Yes, Dad.

His dad stared at his boots and then added, *Nothing wrong with it, though—just that my taste buds are shot, like my liver.*

Darl spent a lot of time at the old lead mine. Sometimes the boy would come over on his trail bike. He'd dismount and they'd squat near each other without saying a word. It smelt strong, even heady up there in the heat . . . assaying the lead tailings, listening to the pasture crackle with the dryness, watching oddly colored sunsets. Sometimes Darl would ask after the boy's dad. *Oh, he's okay,* the boy would say. *He keeps saying his liver's shot and that's why he got sick. When one of his mates rings and tries to get Dad to go out on the piss, he just says, can't mate, doc says my liver's shot.*

After a while, Darl and the boy would hear Pet calling up from the new house—or the "mansion," as the boy called it: *Hey, boys, come down and have something to eat and drink.*

It was as if they were the only people in the world. It would always be like that.

the fireball

★ Geraldton/Greenough

There's a right and a wrong way of doing things, Harold said.

Jenny thought, The right way is usually the wrong way. And if it weren't for the kids . . . She bit her lip, as always.

But Dad, Jim said, those caves are amazing. You should come up and see them. Kangaroos shelter in there during the heat of the day. They are full of white sand that's crumbled from the limestone walls. On top, it's all iron-rock and gravel, with heaps of quartz chips. And the scrub up there is impenetrable. It's all needle tree and dead-finish bushes. And in front of the caves there are great zamia palms. You can see right out across the sandplain paddocks to the ocean.

Harold cut him off, his pained expression saying he'd already been too patient. That's not the point, Jim, it's not our land. Even this isn't our land. Three months we've got, before we have to move back to town. Without the cheap rent, I'd be lucky to cover the renovations at home.

Jim ruminated. His mother held her tongue, as she was expected to do. Eventually she said, It will be interesting

15

catching the school bus into Geraldton, Jim. I guess you'll know a few of the kids.

Not really, said Jim. Most of the upper-school students from out here board at the hostel. But he sparked up, ignoring his father's impatience, and said, There's also a canyon where water runs fast when it rains. Must be some springs down there, because there are clusters of red river-gums. I'll examine it closer tomorrow and take my field notebook.

You'll do no such thing, Jim, said Harold, banging the table ineffectually with the flat of his hand. You stay around this house and go no further.

Jim glanced up at his father with disdain. Old dickhead, he thought. He smiled at his mother and went on eating dinner with exaggerated manners, annoying and pleasing his father at once, who hoped he'd controlled his son.

Susan, Jim's sister, sat opposite, eating slowly and deliberately. She feared the bus, and didn't like this old asbestos, tin-roofed house that was their temporary home. She would be starting high school with the new term, and thought it pretty shoddy that this extra stress was added to her life. Her father didn't bother her too much; she barely thought him worth registering. And she didn't do much that could annoy him. She was a polite young lady. That was all that mattered.

The household's main problem was Harold being home most of the time. He'd taken his long-service leave and spent his days sitting in the front room listening to light classics and reading. Always ready with an opinion, he shouted orders from his seat below the old air-conditioning unit. Hopefully he'll get Legionnaire's disease, said Jim to his mum, and she couldn't help laughing, telling herself Jim didn't mean it.

Jim did try to get through to his father. On a particularly hot day, he went and sat near him in the front room. Waiting until Harold looked up from his page, he spoke quietly so as not to drown out the Ravel gurgling in the background. Dad, there's some zebra finches just outside, you should come and have a look and a listen. They're so chirpy. They live in the needle trees this side of the barbed wire fence. So they're not "out of bounds." Jim even avoided the sarcasm the final comment might carry.

Harold, impervious, said, It's hot out there, son. You'll get filthy traipsing about among the bushes. You should do some of that holiday reading you're supposed to do. Get the jump on your courses.

Already have, Dad. Hey, do you know, there's an echidna that shelters under the house during the heat of the day. Curled up in a ball. It feeds on all those termite mounds down the hill around the melaleuca thickets and York gums.

That's interesting, Jim, said Harold, returning to his book, Ravel louder in his head.

Going out, Jim said to his mother, who was online shopping, muttering at the slow dial-up connection. Going up to the caves, he said. He'd almost given up waiting for a reply when she said, That's fine, darling, wear your hat and take some water.

Jim found Susan sitting on the back step in the shade and asked if she'd like to climb with him. She ignored him and returned to her room to sulk and wait for her turn on "dire-up" so she could get on Facebook. She missed her friends.

Jim loved the cool of the caves.

It's 45 degrees out there and the caves are cool-as, he said to himself. He sketched the vista in his notebook and eyed off the canyon. This island of bushland in a sea of sand, the great stripped areas where the wheat is grown, the sea that joins a deep blue Indian Ocean. He had occasionally gone surfing out there at Flat Rocks with some mates, but surfing wasn't really his thing. He did it because Harold hated it.

He smelt it first. Weird, he thought—like cigarette smoke. Another thing he'd tried but not liked. He was one with Harold on that one.

He hoisted himself up from the sand and the roo-shit and went to the mouth of the cave. Great zamia palm fronds, ancient residues in a place that books told Jim was the most ancient on earth, wavered in the stiffening easterly. It was a searing hot wind rolling off the roof of the outcrops and rushing down into the canyon, and over down towards the house, the sandplains, the sea. He wondered what it would do to the surf when it met that immensity.

He climbed out and onto the top of the cave. A band of smoke rose and capillaried into the wide blue sky a few hills away. It could be mistaken for a dying willy-willy, but the driving easterly, and the continuous feeding of the grey blur against the blue, and the increasingly acrid taste and smell in the air said otherwise.

Jim leapt down through the rocks and crashed into the scrub, scratching and bruising himself as he tumbled towards home. He passed a stand of three primeval-looking trees he'd never seen the like of in nature or a book before, and knew it must be a species verging on extinction. In the rush for home he saw things he'd not seen looking closely, when he'd had an eye to finding. Other than the sound of his exodus, all was silent. The birds had vanished. He tore his flesh plunging through the barbed-wire fence.

Reaching the back steps, he called, Fire! Fire!

He found his mother in the kitchen and said, We must go now, there's fire. She looked out the window, and seeing now a massive wall of flames cascading down from the outcrops, she called, Harold! Harold, we must leave, there's a fire.

Susan yelled, Shit, Mum, what's happening?

Harold walked into the kitchen where the other three had gathered and said, Stop the yelling! What are you panicking about?

Jim grabbed his father's sleeve and dragged him towards the window, pointing at the avalanche of flame, That! That!

Harold picked Jim's hand off his shirt. Settle down, son!

There was an agonizing pause, filled with the rush of wind and flames. They all looked to Harold, who said, Jump in the bath, all of you. Jenny, turn on the shower and put the plug in the bath.

They were nonplussed, so frightened they did what Harold said. Then he vanished and reappeared with blankets, which he soaked under the shower. He threw them over his family, whom, truth be told, he didn't really like. It was a shit of a life. He climbed into the bathtub, where they all crouched, squeezed together with the shower going and wet blankets over their head. Someone was crying, all were shaking, except Harold, who seemed indifferent. There was a whoosh of air like a vacuum cleaner, and the windows lit up orange. The world smelt putrid.

The new house was one of Geraldton's talking points. Susan settled easily into her new role as one of the "wealthy girls," though in truth they had less money than ever. Mortgaged to the hilt, her mother would complain a little too loud, Susan saying, Shoosh, Mum, my friends might hear.

Nouveau-riche status meant little to Jim, but he enjoyed being the center of a different kind of attention. A *Guardian* newspaper reporter had even interviewed him about his experience in The Fires, and Jim had used the occasion to lament the loss of many rare and probably little-known plant species. He called for the preservation of the area, which would certainly bounce back from fire if left untrammelled. He felt that his future as an environmentalist was assured.

When Jim told the story of the fireball that rolled over the tin roof of the house and blazed its way across the sandplain all the way to the ocean, his description was accurate as a naturalist would produce. He researched accounts of fire rolling over roads, across paddocks, and even the iron roofs of houses. Like waves surfing the earth. It made a poet of him. But he didn't mention his father. He almost forgot his father had been there.

carcass

★ Mingenew

The more easygoing among us usually called him "Fossil," but resorted to the standard "Carcass" when one of his more outlandish goals, or "victories," was achieved. And for the purposes of the yarn I am about to relate, he most certainly deserved the name "Carcass."

Carcass was a reasonable shearer, but never a great one. He could knock them off pretty fast, but was, as the cockies say, "rough as guts." The sheep sliding down into his catching pen looked like they'd had a date with a bad surgeon—a plastic surgeon who'd been struck off but kept practicing, nonetheless. Merinos are renowned for the extra wool they carry in their skin folds, and it takes skill to weave the comb in and out of those mighty crevices, but Carcass was notorious for shearing straight on through—skin, wool, and anything else in the way. And he had that element of sadist about him that even the young blokes found a bit hard to stomach. The cockies who knew of him wouldn't let him near their prize rams . . .

I am not one for painting backgrounds, and like to get
to the point. But I will say that like those real estate adverts,
so much rests on location, location, location. Or maybe I
should say isolation, isolation, isolation. I mean, you've got to
understand that when we're shearing the stations, we're a long
way from anywhere, and you tend to get to know each other's
bad habits pretty well. Carcass has many, but his worst as far as
the rest of the blokes are concerned—and I mean any blokes
on the same team as him—is his habit of cracking on to every
girl rouseabout he comes across. They're a captive audience for
him. Sometimes it's a female wool classer, or even the cook. He's
not fussy: any size or shape or age will do. He claims they'll all
fall to his charms sooner or later. Seriously, the guy is grotesque,
and stinks with it. And there you go, he hounds them, flatters
them, jokes with them, drinks with them, smokes dope with
them, and they eventually fall.

Then he'll tell us of his conquest, describe qualities and
flaws with intricate detail, to the point where even the young
blokes don't want to hear anymore. And the fallen girls and
women—they just go red whenever he looks at them, or
anyone else for that matter. Within a day or two, humiliated,
they'll hook a lift with the infuriated contractor, who'll be
muttering to himself, why did I do it, why did I get a girl on
the job? They never think of dropping Carcass, he has that way
about him. Returning, they'll have picked up some young bloke
from God knows where to cover for the girl.

So that's the scenario, repeated over and over. But then
the world turns upside down—for Carcass, for all of us. The
contractor hires this beautiful young woman—sorry if that
sounds off, but she was! I mean, really classy and gorgeous with
it, and with a brain like a steel trap. He hires her because he's
drinking in the pub then playing pool and holding the table
until he's beaten by a chick and can't get over it. And forgetting
about his missus for a moment he asks her if she's looking for
work and she says she might be and he offers her well above the

award and the next thing she's on the team. With his hangover
the next morning he packs his ute and finds her standing at the
passenger's side asking to be let in. He remembers, groans, but
that's it. She's on the team.

The rest of us are already out at the quarters, sorting our
gear out. Sharp-eyed, Carcass sees them coming down the
gravel—Jeez . . . he says. Get a load of that. I'll have her broken
by tomorrow. We look up and see this burst of sunlight that's
not going to fry your brains, and snap back, You'll be lucky,
you dirty bastard. Okay, it's our standard reaction when he
declares an impending conquest.

So she unloads her gear and takes her room—we share two
to a room, but she has her own—and comes out to meet us all.
She's okay. We all like her. She has an easygoing way about her.
But she's so sharp. Carcass drops innuendoes, and she throws
them back at him with a laugh. It'll keep, he says.

The working week begins, and there's no sign of her
breaking. As we watch Carcass's efforts rebuffed with that laugh,
we grow in confidence. Under his watchful eye, as he hacks
the blazes out of a sheep, we banter with her as she sweeps the
board. There's a good feeling on the team for the first time in
months. She has brought heaps of CDs and plays them. Even the
old-timers get into them: the Slits, Sleater-Kinney, shit like that.
The shed pumps. Carcass is clearly in crisis. He's bad-tempered.
Wallops the sheep with his handpiece, which really offends her.
Lay off those sheep! she yells. If you carry on like that I'll report
you to the RSPCA. Now, normally, if someone—anyone—said
something like that, they'd be out on their ear. But she can and
does, and no one holds it against her.

What does she look like? Well, you know, sort of agile, with
smart eyes. A green color. Brown hair. No makeup—that doesn't
work in hot sheds anyway. Melts. But even out of the shed, on
our days off. Just . . . natural. And tall. Leggy, Carcass says, spitting
it out. Three weeks in, and nothing. He's looking hunched, and
"congested." I'm not one for pulling the pud, he says to her, having

now given up on all levels of decency. He'd molest her, we guess, if he thought he could get away with it. But he can't—we'd beat the shit out of him, and he knows it. And she knows it too.

And so the shed comes to an end and the run at that, and with the cutout—a massive piss-up that sees her kiss all us blokes long and hard, and only peck Carcass on the cheek—we jump into the minibus and head back to town to be met by wives and partners, or to be dropped out our places for a few weeks of R&R. Carcass, who always drives the bus, drives even faster than usual. He almost wipes us out three or four times.

During the break, I hook up with the contractor to do a bit of cockie shearing. He has a few sheds not too far from town that really only need him classing, me shearing, and the farmers' sons penning up. Easy, not pressure work, and I build up my nest egg that little bit further. Some of the others say I'm hungry, but I don't give a shit. One day I'll have that big house and pay for it with cash. So after we knock off one evening, we drive to the local pub for a quick drink, and run into Carcass. His misery has worn off by this stage, and he shouts us a round, which is not a common thing. We ask him how he's been and if he's still celibate, and he just laughs it off and says that you win some and you lose some. But he can't quite hold it together because after a few seconds he adds . . . not that I lose many. Then he insists that our contractor make sure a less bitchy female rousy is taken on for the next run, as he has to get his tally back up. So we laugh for longer than we mean to, and finally decide to kick off. We're moving to another shed the next day.

Where? asks Carcass.

At Ben Williams's, we say.

Well, I'll be damned, he comes back. That's where I'm staying. The old bloke has a shack down the back of the place and I've just moved in.

The contractor is incredulous. You mean you've given up that swish place you've got in town? Given up your plasma telly and gas barbie?

Nah, says Carcass, this is a temporary arrangement, it just suits me at the moment.

I look hard at Carcass, who seems more decrepit than usual. His bulkiness shifts uneasily on his legs, and the hairs in his nose are so barbed that they're pricking his mucous membranes. He hasn't washed for days. He's sweating grime.

Anyway, he adds, as we're leaving, poke your head down when you finish work and I'll give you a drink.

Two acts of generosity in two days, that's overload.

We don't see Carcass while we're working. We check with Ben Williams regarding the location of his shack, and he says it's about a mile down the creek. He is a flat kind of bloke, so he doesn't offer to discuss how he came to this strange arrangement with Carcass. He just goes off to make sure the sheep penning's going according to plan.

To tell the truth, we really just want to head home. The sheep are tough—a lot of sand in the wool—and I've been through a lot of cutters. I'll be grinding all night to get them right for the next day. But victims of Carcass that we ultimately are, we drive down the track along the creek to search out the shack. It's easy enough to find, and Carcass is already out the door when we arrive.

Good onya for comin' down, he says. Or gloats. We've seen that look in his eyes all too often. They're semi-closed and almost weeping. He fixes us with a boar-like intensity. Like he's going to charge.

Come in, come in.

We follow him, at a safe distance. And there she is, slightly blushing, flipping the top of a longneck. A beer, guys? she asks.

Er, thanks. We look at Carcass—glowing . . . no, swollen with vindication . . . we look at *her* . . . ?

What? She cuts in before we can speak: Carcass had no place to stay, you know, and Ben's my uncle, so I can use this place whenever I'm around.

We shuffle our feet and say nothing. Carcass just has that big grin on his face that says, You guys keep your mouths shut.

Well, she says, anyway, there's room here.

We look around. There isn't much room. The lounge is a double bed folded up for the day. There doesn't seem to be much more than a kitchen. An outside dunny?

We have a drink, make our excuses, and leave. I make the foolish mistake of glancing back as we drive off along the creek. Carcass is at the door, giving us and anything else that might walk, crawl, slither, or fly past the thumbs up. Yep, all's right in the world.

mange

★ Dalwalinu

The seven-year itch. Sarcoptic mange. Microscopic parasites. Sarcoptes mites. Laying their waste on the skin, inside hair follicles. Secondary infections. Hair loss. Foxes plead for warmth, and wander in the full-blown light of day. A daylight foxstrike on the road.

I can't say the doctor visibly retreated when the old man told him he'd had mange for years, but I think he wanted to. I could be projecting here. There'd be a battery of psychoanalytical terms for my response, but I've little faith in them. My ECG machine went wild as I hoisted myself up to listen, so I called out, It's okay, I'm just shifting myself . . . knowing the doctor would turn his attention to me and the nurses come running. I might not die that night, but I could.

Otherwise, I was fairly compos, if a little vague and racked by constant shaking. But this conversation, between the earnest young South African doctor and the wizened but zesty old wheatbelt farmer, was something I wanted to listen to—living or dead, I reckon I had a vested interest in its progress, and that rather than eavesdropping I was, by juxtaposition, a concerned party. After all, I might come back as a mange-ridden red fox, or spread mange to my loved ones as they mourned over my corpse. I remembered my wife telling me that yoga sessions usually begin and end with the corpse posture. That helped.

Anyway, as far as I can remember, the conversation between doctor and patient went along the following lines. Bear in mind that the whole time it was going on, the doctor was trying unsuccessfully to tap a vein in the old man's arm, to draw blood for tests pertaining to the *unrelated* condition— *not* mange, that is—that had brought him to the hospital in the first place:

It's because of the foxes. Up on the farm. Terrible creatures.

Yes. Yes.

If you've seen what they do to a coop of chickens if they get in—sampling the livers and little else—you'd agree.

Yes. Yes. Sorry, another *small* pinprick in the arm. Having a little trouble finding a vein. (I smiled at this—I love medical tautologies.)

My veins have always been like that. I used to shoot dozens of foxes in a night. Hunt them. I have to say I enjoyed it. Enjoyed killing the killers. (Truly, his laugh after this was a cackle.)

Yes. Yes. Hmmm, they *are* killers. Hmmm . . . Ohhhh, no luck there, sorry. Sorry about the bruises—you'll have some beauties. We'll have to try the other arm.

That's okay. Whatever it takes. I used to shoot them *and* skin them. I was the fastest skinner in the district. It's what I most miss. We've been off the farm for ten years. We farmed out on the edge of the wheatbelt. Far as you can go. Some paddocks— and these paddocks were thousands of acres—we could only crop every few years because it was so dry. But foxes! They were everywhere. I shot them only in the head if I could, to avoid damaging the pelts. But I'd happily have shot them where it hurts most first. That's something to be said for the mangy bastards—sorry for my French—didn't matter where you shot them, their pelts were useless.

The doctor was hypnotized by the old codger's ingrown veins and barely uh-hummed back.

It didn't matter where you shot 'em! Sometimes if I was feelin' down or off-color, I'd spread poison. That's another story—plenty of punishment for the devils there, but not as much reward for the hunter.

Yes. Yes. Think we're onto a vein here.

It was them foxes that gave me the mange.

Maybe this time. Now, another pinprick. No, wait—sorry. (He almost said, Damn, I could sense it.)

That's okay. You'll get one in the end. Yes, I've had the mange for twenty years. Can't get rid of it.

Hmmm. (The doctor had lifted his head and broken the spell; he seemed slightly bothered, outside the vein horror.) I know humans can catch mange, but it's easy to clear up and doesn't last long.

Nope, sorry, Doc, the specialist (he said this with particular emphasis) said I would have it *forever.* Them mites love me. Just love me. Stay buried in my body, gettin' born again!

He laughed loud and irritated the doctor, who'd convinced himself he was just about to strike it rich, and only missed because the old man's body shook as he laughed.

Look, here's a patch. Look, if I scratch it, it flakes. Gets infected easily.

Please try not to move your arm, Mr. R. It is quite difficult to get a vein. I will mention your situation regarding the apparent "mange" to our skin specialist, and he can take a look at you. If you're not around mangy foxes now, it should be easy enough to clear up. You don't have any pets with mange?

Pets? Waste of time. Always had working dogs on the farm for the sheep, but they lived outside. Never let a dog inside. Couldn't stand them touching me. Never liked them. Wouldn't even let them in the cab of the ute. I've gotta say, though, there's nothing as beautiful as a clean fox fur—I used to say to my wife that it was as good as touching her!

I almost laughed out loud but held it in. It might kill me and kill the conversation. The monologue. I was learning stuff. I should tell you now that I've more than a vested interest. More than a fear of catching the mange. I have been campaigning for years to have the local annual fox-cull competition banned. Brutality. I wasn't quite sure how, but this was invaluable info.

Look, Mr. R., I just can't find a vein, sorry. I think I will have to ask a nurse to take blood from you.

Yes, those nurses do a lot of it, Doc. Sure you don't want to touch this mange? Might be educational for you.

Probably not a good idea, Mr. R. I'll mention it to the specialist.

No need, there's no cure. It's just part of my identity. And every time it flares and I itch I remember the farm. And these mite things are the offspring of the mites that were there when I was there. And maybe they trace their heritage right back to Europe. That's where my ancestors came from, Germany. But they came here in the 1910s to make a life for themselves. They were never no Nazis. Just hardworking German country folk. They have red foxes there, too. Terrible creatures, foxes. Eat the livers out of chickens. Will kill twenty and sample them all and then leave the carcasses strewn about like slaughter.

I'll go now, Mr. R., and find a nurse to take your blood.

Nothing like a fox in the spotlight.

The nurse came in after a while, but the old man didn't say much more. He flirted with her a bit, but it seemed the fox stuff was a man's business. The nurse had drawn the diaphanous curtain fully between us, so I couldn't really see anything (should I have been trying to look?), but I could paint the picture through his cackling, his broken but vivid words. He was a master of semitones. The doctor scuttled in to ask the nurse how it was going, and then scuttled out. I shifted in my bed again, enough to set off the ECG alarm. It's okay, it's okay, just adjusting myself. It sounded odd, but no one poked their head in.

The following morning saw me slightly better, and the old man chipper. Is that the word used for one of German heritage? Bright-eyed and bushy-tailed seems nondenominational, but still pertinent in the context. I was amusing myself in small-minded ways. I hadn't slept for a long time. Bright-eyed and bushy-tailed? A nurse swept the curtain back and said, Mr. L., meet Mr. R.—you have been neighbors for a while.

Mr. R. immediately said, Gidday, but I averted my eyes. Such confrontation couldn't work for me. I already knew him as Mr. R.—he was always being called Mr. R. I knew him as Mr. R., fox-killing psychopath. I didn't want a relationship with him. I didn't want to open a dialogue! I averted my eyes, grumbled, and pointed to the ECG. The nurse swept around our beds, indifferent. I've got mange, Mr. R. said, but he might have been saying this to the nurse, who it turns out was just back from a two-week holiday and knew nothing of either Mr. R. or me, other than what our medical notes showed. We were clean slates for him.

By the next day I was able to chat and receive visitors. Mr. R.'s skin specialist hadn't materialized, and I tried to hint to each of "my people" that my neighbor might have something horrifically contagious. He no longer tried speaking to me, but spoke to my visitors with enthusiasm. No matter how much I tried to signal them with hand movements and grimaces, they all replied to him. My sister even sat next to him for a while. My ECG went up and the nurses asked everyone to leave me to rest. I could have sworn I saw Mr. R. smirk. I certainly heard him cackle.

I slept long that night. For the first time in days. When I woke, Mr. R. was gone. Nurses were wheeling a new, crisply made bed into the place where he and his bed and his mange had bubbled. My curiosity surprised me. Where is Mr. R.? I asked. I was expecting to hear he died during the night, of the ailment that had brought him there; or maybe the mange had finished him off. My heart raced, and the nurses commented on the spike—not enough to set the alarm off, but getting there. And you were seeming so much better, one said. I was afraid Mr. R. had died. I really was.

Mr. R.? Well, he's gone home. Left early this morning, just after I took your vitals. Don't you remember? He even said good-bye.

I didn't. Nothing. A blank.

But my heart settled, and I stared at the ceiling. Then the alarm went off and the nurses started fussing. Foxes! I yelled. Nothing else. Though deep inside my head I could feel the mange at work—and I knew Mr. R. was out there already spreading the mange, sharing the love. It was his God-appointed duty.

the cartesian diver

> "So you're the diviner now," Tom said. "I might
> have seen it coming."—Randolph Stow, *Tourmaline*

★ Westonia

*I have been a country boy as well, you know. I have known
the dry . . . In the hard times when there was little work I went back out
there, conjuring up a living . . .*

It had been a drier year than usual in a very dry place. So
dry that farmers hadn't even bothered putting in crops over the
autumn and winter. The dams were empty, and wells drawn on,
to the point of insolvency, windmills turning hard in the blazing
easterlies that came in daily. House tanks were filled with water
trucked from standpipes, and only the wealthiest had kept their
patches of lawn green in defiance, standing their ground in the
face of suffering. Herds of cattle and flocks of sheep had been
culled to bare bones, to basal metabolic rate, as the town doctor
joked—and he spent most of his time propping up the wettest
place in town, the front bar of the pub. He had a sick wit.

There was only one church in town, and that was Anglican,
though it was hard to guess that because it did business for a

number of creeds. Even Catholics turned up there occasionally—though they mainly traveled to a neighboring town also in the grip of drought, whose baptismal font was equally dusty. The few Church of Christ believers in the district worshipped in their houses—you could tell a prayer meeting was in swing by whose cars were gathered along the verges. The "C of C" tended to be town dwellers there, not so much farmers, though there were one or two C of C families with big spreads. When the meetings were at those farms, the others in town didn't really know, or didn't *really* care, because it's true that gravel roads exact their own kinds of surveillance. But in town itself, gatherings were always kept an eye on, or out for, though none was sure why. Wherever and however they prayed, it was as dry for them as any other, as dry for each and every one of them. No prayers from anywhere would bring rain. The town had signed off on that with spiritual totality. It had ceased to believe in moisture.

Then a lay preacher, a self-styled Man of God, turned up on a corner of the main street and began to proselytize. This corner was opposite the bank, just outside the hardware store. The preacher was full of the sins of the townsfolk, and full of humanity's evil, making a clear link between the dry and their neglect of God. He might have been run out of town by all and sundry, but his promise of rain, of water, eventually struck a note. On the first day he was ignored; on the second he was abused; on the third he was listened to. A crowd blocked the main street, and traffic came to a standstill. He plied his message a fourth and a fifth and a sixth day.

Where he went after he finished his preaching, no one knew. He arrived early in the morning and set off at sunset, subsisting on a bottle of water and little else. He never seemed to flag or weaken under the sun. His hat was gnarled. He always came from the north, and headed back that way. No one thought of going after him—at first. But curiosity and hope got the better of them, and at the end of the sixth day they started following him when his sermonizing came to an end. They followed him north to his bush camp about five miles along the road. And there they stood by him and watched his every action until he said: Return at dawn and I will show you the truth of water. The liquid science of God!

Word spread quickly that evening and through the night. Such a crowd gathered that the scrub was trampled and damaged, and nobody cared. There must have been a hundred people arcing around the preacher, including the Anglican minister, the doctor (who looked sober and solemn), and the mayor. The town policeman was there, but not in uniform. I don't go on duty until 8 a.m., he said.

The preacher still lay in his swag, but irritated by the crowd. He tossed and turned. He belched and grunted. Suddenly he went still, as if in a trance, staring at the dawn sky. Around him, a half dozen bottles of water—old two-liter lemonade bottles clearly filled with water. One of them near the supine preacher's head was three-quarters empty. What he'd suckled on throughout the night, the townsfolk guessed. And just as the crowd's impatience and agitation increased, clearly discernible as the scrub crackled with the snapping of brush underfoot, drowning out the birdlife, the preacher rose, dressed in rags, and spread his hands to the dawn, to the crowd. I am surrounded by water! he called, pointing one by one to the bottles of water strewn about. God filled these containers through prayer and conviction. My prayer and conviction. Imagine how many containers we might fill if you take him into your heart and pray with me!

There was a long pause as the sun rose and made things colder, though no less dusty. The crowd stared at the beatified man. He spoke: Once I was a teacher of physics, and it came to me during a demonstration to my students that *I* was a vessel waiting to be filled with the love of God, just as these vessels, these bottles around me, were waiting and then were filled. Observe a truth. I will take one of these bottles and introduce this small tube into the liquid . . .

The preacher, looking like Professor Julius Sumner Miller, went to a pocket in his rags and removed a tube closed at one end and open at the other, which he showed slowly and carefully to the gathering, instilling it with light and power. He filled it partly with water from the bottle that had been three-quarters drunk. He then uncapped a full bottle and submerged the tube through the neck, licking at the drops of life-giving water that spilled from the bottle as the tube was submerged. He then recapped the bottle and held the water bottle high, allowing the sun to fill it with strong prismatic rays, and all watched on as the tube bobbed near the top of the bottle, hanging there suspended.

This, said the preacher, is a Cartesian diver! Now: as God squeezes our world, so this tube suspended in this bottle, our body—our individual bodies and our collective souls—responds! He squeezed the bottle, and the tube descended to the bottom. He dramatically released some of the pressure of his handgrip, and the tube ascended. He then worked his grip so that the "diver" hovered midway in the world of water, in our bodies, our souls. Holding the bottle aloft for a good while, he said, Go now—this is the way. Herein flows your water. You will never thirst again.

Astonishingly, the crowd dispersed. Each walked off silently toward town, carrying the news of their witnessing. Those who had driven left their cars and walked towards town. Even the policeman left his car there by the side of the road, near the bush camp, unlocked.

The preacher did not appear in town that day. In the evening all went back to the camp expecting to hear more good news. The skies remained as dry as ever, but they knew something was coming, something was due. They *believed*. But there was no sign of the preacher or even that he'd ever been there. Just the traces of where they'd walked and stood, crushing the scrub. It would be true to say, however, that the consequences of his visitation were fundamental, pivotal to the fate of that dry town so run down by a drier year than usual, when God seemed to have evaporated. A fate deep in the well of themselves they welcomed, ecumenically.

memorial

★ Beacon

One of the last towns before the desert, certainly the last town which might *just* be described as belonging to the "wheatbelt." The far far northeastern boundary, out where the dusty broad-acres meet the scrub, where the rain falls more on what was once the drier side of the fence where the scrub still exists, than the side closer to the "weather," long cleared to bare bones. Crops worth harvesting only once every four or five years. Mainly sheep grazing, thin, with burrs in their wool. Gnarled creatures, tough to shear. With independent minds and wills that are determined to thwart farmer and shearer alike. Anyone worth their salt would admire them.

The scrub around here is one of the final refuges for mallee fowl. Only a few meters in and you might well see a nesting mound. Remarkable things. Further out, the mining companies. Further out still, the "native reserve" land: you need a permit to go there, and it makes the small-town whites shitty and jealous. There is only one Aboriginal family in town itself, and they pass muster only because the father and two of his sons are gun shearers and are in high demand. As a rule, shearers don't travel out that way if they can avoid it. The town itself is small even by small-town standards. A general store, a pub, a post office, the town hall, a primary school, shire offices, a few dozen houses. There was once a district high school, but that has closed, and all the older kids catch the bus forty k's to the next town, or else board hundreds of k's away. Most are happy to leave.

At the center of the town, near the town hall, is a memorial park. It is the pride of the town, and precious fresh water is dumped on a small patch of grass and garden surrounding the war memorial there. Many of the more respectable locals in the district call it "our little oasis." More fertilizer, insecticide, herbicide, water-retaining granules, and water itself are poured on that patch than on the entire footy oval at Subiaco, way down in the city where the Eagles, this town's preferred AFL team, play. Even their own footy oval—and footy is the sport of the district—is a dustbowl with gimlet trunks, warped and wobbling, painted a rough white, as goalposts. Neither are the houses upright, mostly jerry-built out of iron and asbestos. A few old stone buildings from the earliest days are so roughly hewn, they give the impression of being bent and buckled even if, according to the spirit level, they're not. The few trees left surrounding the town are gnarled and stunted.

In fact, as a visiting wit said, to the memory of all in the pub one night, just before the captain of the football team punched him out, "Your bloody war memorial is the only tall, straight thing in this town." It was confirmed by all the men and women present that there was something sexually sick in what the visitor was suggesting.

"The little oasis" is much loved. Not just for the green glimmer of civilization which both allures and torments the townsfolk, but also for that war memorial. On it are the names of those who have fallen in three wars. Four during the First

World War, which came only ten years after the town was founded and the district "opened up," six from the Second World War, and one from Vietnam. Strangely, every surname is the same. All of the same family. A powerful, respected family in the district. The pioneers. As three of the commemorated have the first name "Reginald," rather than the family being called by surname, they are known as the "Reggies." And that's not just in terms of the dead, but also the living of the family. Male or female, they are the "Reggies." The male Reggies are shire presidents and heads of the local Country Party, they sit on rural and other official boards and committees; the females have been at the head of the local CWA from its foundation through to the present day. The patriarch of the family, the oldest man in town, is known as Captain Reggie, and is the most revered figure for a vast distance, it is believed.

Captain Reggie is ancient. He is in his nineties, and served in North Africa with the AIF during the Second World War. Later he was in New Guinea. Fought the Krauts and the Japs, he says. And people listen. No Kraut nor Jap would be welcome in their town, and given it's so far off the beaten track, not even the odd tourist in a Budget rent-a-car ("No Birds"!) turns up. Not until today, that is, and what a day to turn up. It's ANZAC Day and Captain Reggie is in uniform and medals and Dawn Service has been and gone and he is still at the Oasis telling his tales when the No Birds car turns up. Strange time to arrive. They must have been staying in a neighboring town.

So out steps a Japanese woman—a young woman—from the passenger's side, then another young woman from the driver's side. Captain Reggie has a sharp eye and spots them first. He points shakily with his walking stick, and the other Reggies (young and older), and many others, follow the line of his stick, jolting with surprise when they see the young women.

Japs! spits Captain Reggie. It's sixty years but I know Japs when I see 'em.

Not knowing how to react, those around him just watch and listen. The visitors have come nearer to the crowd, curious maybe. One of them speaks to Captain Reggie, who is shaking with anger.

Hello, the driver says. Captain Reggie is silent. She says, You *must* be Captain Reggie. We were told by the man who owns the hotel in X that we'd find you here today.

The townspeople form a circle around the visitors. Not quite a menacing circle, but the women are entirely surrounded, with Captain Reggie at the eye of the storm, beside the War Memorial. What do you want? Captain Reggie fumes.

We have brought a letter from our great-uncle who died early this year. He asked us to come to this town on this day and to hand it to you.

The driver removes a letter from her handbag and the crowd jumps back. A gun? A knife? They are not sure why the caution, the fear, rushes over them. They are a tough community. It's just for a split second, then they relax. Captain Reggie shakes but remains still, his anger overwhelming all other thoughts and reactions.

The woman holds the letter out and Captain Reggie does nothing.

Please, sir, take the letter. It is from our great-uncle who said it is important you receive this. We have come a long way.

Captain Reggie knocks the letter to the ground with his stick, and the woman snatches her hand back. The passenger, unperturbed, leans down and picks the letter up. Some of the CWA women notice that she does so with grace. They push this to the back of their minds, where the thought is less offensive. She holds the letter out, and Captain Reggie knocks it to the ground again. The crowd is silent and nonplussed. Maybe they will attack the women and not know why. Tear them to shreds and bury them out beside a mallee fowl mound in the scrub. A dog barks distantly and the wind picks up, knocks hats off, disturbs the visitors' immaculate hair, then drops away to nothing. The letter flutters away.

Captain Reggie's great-grandson is his favorite. He is only five and curious with it. He's a sparky child with goodwill towards everyone and everything. He wears glasses and is obsessed with numbers. He counts sheep, he counts cars, anything at all. He likes things to be orderly. The boy rushes in, breaking the crowd's self-restraint, and captures the letter. He takes the letter towards Captain Reggie, hesitates, and hands it back to the women. They both reach out and grip it at the same time. And in a single movement they hold it towards the old man again. Flustered, he lowers his stick and reaches for it with his other hand. He pushes it into his top pocket, struggles up, and begins to walk off. The crowd files slowly behind him, and none looks back as the visitors make their way to "No Birds," get into the car, and drive off from whence they came, never to be seen in the town again.

The youth of the town, as in so many outback towns, often find themselves collectively bored. Admittedly, there's not a lot to do. There is no theater, only a service station café, and limited sport facilities. When the footy season isn't on, there's pretty well nothing happening entertainment-wise. Strangely, it's never been a cricket town. May be something to do with the eviscerating summers. And though there's only one pub, with a wary publican (who won't have rock bands or even a jukebox), and most trouble in the town is caused by young people drunk, it seems they have a never-ending supply of booze. They get drunk, run amok, and depress their elders. Still, their elders did it when they were young too. Soon the teenage girls are pregnant and they marry the farm boys young. It ensures dynasties, that land stays locked up between the same families. There's sense to it, they say.

So when the town awakes to the following morning and finds the war memorial and the oasis besmeared with red paint, they think some of their young have had too much and lost their minds. But even this is hard to accept. To violate the war memorial on ANZAC Day, or just after, has no precedent in town, in the district, nor within three hundred kilometers.

Searching their combined soul, it is not long before a voice rises above the angry and wailing crowd, It was the Japs!

The shire president takes responsibility. Before calling the police, who are fifty k's away in B, he will speak with Captain Reggie to see if he can offer any advice on the matter. Yes! Yes! The letter. They've all been talking about the letter. Some of the Reggies implored the captain to read it, to tell them what it was about, but he took it home and locked it away. He wouldn't be drawn on the matter and was so out of sorts, so cranky, that they eventually let him be. But the town was abuzz with it. And now this!

Stop! the shire president calls, his face red with frustration. Don't clean it off, the police will need to see it. Don't touch anything. But it is too late—in the split second that his attention was turned elsewhere, the townswomen and their men have started at the paint with anything they have to hand. Even as they hear him, they continue. But it's deep-set and it will take more than shirtsleeves and elbow grease to remove. It will be solvents and scrubbing brushes and replanted lawn. The gravity of the crisis overwhelms them.

I'll shoot the bitches, one man yells.

They should have wiped the country off the planet, the head of the CWA, wife of the shire president, shrieks.

The shire president seeks to regain control—he is a Reggie, of course, and is embarrassed by his wife's brutality. The Reggies are the measure of strength *and* reason. If they can't hold it together when the crunch comes, who will?

Stop! he calls. The clue will be in Captain Reggie's letter. I will go and see him.

Which he does.

Captain Reggie looks at the crowd through his window. It was a mistake moving into town from the farm, he thinks. The shire president, his grandson, knocking on the door. He hesitates, then opens the door a crack.

Just you, not the rest, he says, and lets him in.

Captain Reggie, the memorial has been vandalized, says the shire president.

Yes, what of it? the old man barks.

The shire president is so taken by surprise that he repeats himself.

Stop gibbering, says Captain Reggie.

It is suddenly so silent, inside and outside, that the shire president knows they're in the eye of the storm. The real storm. The big one.

We think those Japs came back late at night or in the early morning and did it, says the shire president.

Captain Reggie rubs the valleys of white whiskers on his chin, his eyes red in their lipid oceans tormented with warfare. Shut up, you fool. You're all fools. And stop looking at me like that. Holier than thou. We're all fools, sitting out here thinking over our empire. Our land of the rising sun.

The shire president shifts uneasily. He is standing but wants to sit. He suddenly agrees with his wife that he needs to lose weight. Time slows down, and he sees the house he is standing in for the first time. Everything is decrepit. The patriarch of the town is living in refuse. Why hasn't he—why haven't we—noticed? We never come in here, he thinks. And Captain Reggie stinks of urine. He is filthy. The president steadies himself and says, What was in the letter, Captain Reggie? I am going to ring the police, and I need to let them know what's what.

Shut up, you dunce. You won't ring the police. Just shut up and clean the place up and go about your business. Nothing will change.

The police will demand that letter, Captain Reggie.

Why, are you going to tell them about it?

Someone will.

Why? Forget about it. Show some respect to an old man and forget about it. Keep the police out of it. Anyway . . . I have destroyed the letter. I shouldn't have taken it in the first place.

So that's that. And Captain Reggie has his way and the town remains quiet. Strangely, he stops grinding his teeth over the Krauts and the Japs as the town spends more and more time denouncing them. The Krauts and the Japs become as one in the town's hatred. The Aboriginal residents in and out of town notice they are less maligned than before. They are tempted to say something bad about the Japs, but they don't. They keep to themselves and do their work in the sheds.

Not too long after the "incident," Captain Reggie dies. The shire president and his wife clean up his house and are repulsed by what they find—food rotting under the bed, a toilet so filthy it has to be fumigated. They half hope the letter still exists, and that Captain Reggie was having them on about destroying it. But there's no sign.

They do find a strange photo, though—one they don't really understand and don't exert any energy trying to understand. It was clearly taken after the war. Captain Reggie has his arm around an emaciated Japanese soldier. Both men are smiling. The shire president remarks that only their five-year-old ever received a smile as warm as that from Captain Reggie. Stern old bastard, truth be had.

Thought he ruled the town, his wife adds, almost vehemently. She brushes something unpleasant from her dust coat as she says this.

It looks like an Allied prisoner-of-war camp somewhere, and the Japanese soldier is just being released. Written on the back is: "Lest we forget." The shire president instinctively screws up the photo, tosses it in an open green garbage bag at his feet, and moves on to the next bit of rubbish cluttering the deceased's bureau. As night falls, they reach the final uncleared corner of the back sleep-out. The lighting is poor, so they don't really register the exact tone of the empty cans of red paint they collect to throw in the back of the trailer with the rest of the rubbish. Then again, maybe they do. Maybe they do.

a load of bricks

★ Koorda

When we needed to build on, the boys having long waited for separate rooms, it didn't surprise me that Bob said he'd build it himself. That's the kind of fella he is, my husband. And when he said he'd take the truck down to the city and collect the bricks himself, it was also to be expected. Bob hasn't changed much since we married, and probably long before that. Forty years later, with a heart condition, and after all the tragedy we've shared, he's much the same. If you want a job well done, then do it yourself, he says. Everybody says this, but Bob really means it. He always follows through. He always means what he says.

I remember the morning he set out. Vividly. It was winter, and there was a glassy sheen over the crops. Not a serious frost, but a little worrying all the same. The skies were silver-blue, and I wished we had more trees around the house paddock to hide us from the vast aching expanse of the farm. Bob said he'd be back by midnight. I wish you'd sleep over at Mum's, I said—it's too much to drive down and back in a day. And it is—a good four hours down plus loading time. And that's four hours in a car; it takes even longer in a truck, especially a semi, and there's that crazy city traffic to negotiate. Mum's place was on the edge of the city, on the road north . . . he could be up at the crack of dawn and home late morning. But no, Bob would do it his way. Bob can be pigheaded like that.

When it struck midnight and Bob wasn't back, I knew something was wrong. I switched on the lights, which were dim because I hadn't run the generator long in the evening and the storage batteries were low. I wandered through to the lounge room to the mantelpiece clock that had chimed so loud and clear. I tapped the face of it, hoping I'd misheard, that it was really around eleven. I tapped it hoping it had gone wrong, that the hands would wind backwards with gentle encouragement. If anyone other than Bob had been this late, I wouldn't have worried, but he's so precise. Midnight was the outer limit. If all was okay, he'd be back in the house and waking me up even if he wasn't trying to. I put a trunk call through to Mum to see if he'd dropped by there. She wasn't too happy to be woken at that "ungodly" hour! No, haven't seen him, darl. Sorry. Don't worry. I knew I'd be up for the rest of the night, so I took a torch, went out to the engine shed, and fired up the generator. It was relief to kick the crank, never my favorite job. Back inside the house, I lit the kitchen stove, made myself a cuppa, and tried to get warm.

As time ticked on, I poked my head into the boys' room to see how they were—Chris was half-hanging out of his bed and looked like an icicle. It was really cold in there. So I tucked him back in, and he half-woke, asking if Dad was home. Not yet, but soon, I soothed, and he instantly went back to sleep. Adjusting the curtains, because the moonlight was cutting in over their faces, I looked out over the wheat crop, a grey-blue in the harsh night light. I could see the black line of the road that comes down to the farmhouse, and I watched and listened for a good while, but there was nothing.

At first light, just before the children got out of bed, Bob arrived home. I've lost the trailer, he said. I made him a cuppa. He was filthy. I've got to head back down to clear up the mess. . . . It'll take the front-end loader to sort it out. Why don't you ask Billy to give you a hand, Bob? I pleaded, knowing he'd say no. Billy is his best friend, and he's always telling Bob that best friends help each other out, that it's not one-way traffic. Bob's always looking to lend Billy a hand but can't cope if it comes back the other way. He just doesn't like owing a favor, as he puts it, even to his best mate. If you were trying to help Bob avoid being struck by lightning, he'd give you the brush-off. No need, mate, I'm right.

The kids clamored around their dad, asking what was wrong. Nothing, boys, just lost the trailer with some bricks. Most of them were stacked on the main tray and they're just fine. Have to go back down to clean up the mess and save the bricks that aren't broken. Hopefully recover a few packs. Otherwise it'll be another drive to the city to make up the shortfall. Bob always spoke to the boys as men.

Where are the bricks? Where is the trailer? How did it happen? Are there bricks on the road? Will cars hit them? Will there be accidents? the boys asked at a canter, furiously excited. Kid-like, not man-like.

Nothing to worry about, boys, and there are no bricks on the road . . . they're down a culvert. What's a culvert, Dad? they asked. A big ditch along the side of the road. Now, you get ready for school because I've got to head on down to Mack's Crossing to sort it out. Mack's Crossing was the family name for a road crossing about twenty miles south of Koorda. The farm that surrounded the crossing belonged to Mack Devlin, who'd been best man at our wedding though he and Bob had long since fallen out. It'd always got to Billy, really offended him, that Bob had chosen Mack over himself to be best man. Mack's not even a close friend, he'd declared. But Mack *was* captain of the footy team and Bob thought that made it right:

showed respect to *my* status, to the status of *our* marriage in the community. Won't feel any more indebted to him than I do when I play footy under him, Bob said at the time. And that's what it was really all about.

After Bob went to shower, and I started cutting the boys' lunches, Chris, our older boy, came up and asked me if he could go with his dad to help out. I am old enough, he said. But you've got school, Chris, and, what's more, you know Dad likes to look after things himself. Then how am I supposed to ever learn anything? said Chris, school banished from his thinking. And I'm his son . . . he'd want his son there . . . being his son makes it different. I am not really sure how, I said, half to myself.

And then, before I knew it, Bob comes to me with a towel around his waist, looking burnt from a too-hot shower—it was still cold despite the kitchen Metters burning away—and said, I think I'll take Chris with me. Has he been at you? I asked, slightly annoyed but knowing in truth Chris had gone straight to his room to dress for school and had had no time to intercept his father. No, no . . . boy didn't say anything . . . seems the time is right. He's a chip off the old block . . . or will be.

Our younger boy, Peter, at first clamored to go as well, but he wasn't *really* interested, and let it drop. In fact, Peter wanted to get to the school bus as soon as possible, worried about missing it, not that *he'd* ever missed it. He was giving news first up and was excited about showing the class a sun skink he'd disturbed when splitting wood for the lounge-room fire. He'd scooped the sun skink up and placed it in a shoebox with flywire over the top—the poor thing looked half stunned and still sleepy with cold to me, wrenched out of its hibernation. Normally I wouldn't have let him take it to be tortured with enthusiasm at school, but it seemed a better fate than burning as it could have, given where he'd found it. And Peter was sure to look after it and bring it home unscathed—he was the naturalist of the family.

So Peter raced out of the house, grabbing his lunch on the way and kissing me so quickly I barely felt his lips on my cheek. Calling out good-bye and good luck to his brother and father, he peeled his bike off the side of the house with a nimble movement, shoebox precarious but ultimately safe in his lap with one hand resting on it, the other hand on the handlebars, a heavy bag on his shoulders, riding off fast down the endlessly long driveway to the watertank on its side that Bob had placed up on the main road to serve as family bus shelter. The way he did this was a miracle I felt fortunate to witness, as I always did.

Bob and Chris headed down to the machinery shed not long after Peter had vanished. Have to unload the bricks still on the truck, then secure the loader on the tray, said Bob. You can watch and learn, Chris. Then after popping back into the house to collect some food I'd packed, they were off to Mack's Crossing. As they went out the door, Chris turned back to look at me, grinning from ear to ear. I blew him a kiss and felt good for him. It was as if his whole life had been lived to get to this point. I thought to myself, Bob, you can be an insensitive clot sometimes, but in the end you'll come through. Nothing wrong with making a kid wait. For the first time in many years, I thought, I'll cook the boys up a treat tonight not because they expect me to, but because I *want* to. I even gave Billy a call and told him Bob was taking Chris with him to help clean up a mess Bob had made! Billy was silent for a long while on the other end of the phone.

By mid to late-ish afternoon, by the time Peter was home with his lizard and full of news of his news, it was quite warm— unseasonably warm, as they say. I took off my jumper and fed Peter scones and juice and listened to the day's doings. The lizard was a hit, and seemed no worse for wear; its blood having heated up, it was skittering around the box. Now let it go somewhere it can sneak in and stay warm till spring, I said. Where's Chris and Dad? he eventually asked, conscious of the warmish, gaping silence about him. I didn't feel like hiding something bad, so I said, I don't know . . . I expected them back for a late lunch. Your dad took some scones and fruit and a thermos . . . you know he likes to eat. And Chris! We smiled at each other—a joke between mother and younger son.

When dinnertime came and I had a big spread on the table with just an increasingly agitated Peter and myself sitting there in the half-light, peering up the gravel driveway, I really started to worry.

I got up from the table, Peter's eyes anxiously following me, and said, through the back of my head, I'll phone Uncle Billy.

Hi, Billy, it's me again. One of those days. No sign of Bob . . . should have been back hours ago. I've a bad feeling about this just like I did last night, and I was right then. Ring Mack, Billy replied after I filled in missing details. You know I can't do that, Billy. You know that. Yes, Billy *knew* why. Another uncomfortable silence before Billy responded distantly, I'll ring Mack, don't worry. I knew that if Billy rang Mack it'd be the end of his friendship with Bob. Bob was cut and dried about those things. This time I stayed silent. Bye, said Billy, but before he hung up he said rapidly, you've got to wonder about him losing those bricks at Mack's Crossing. I mean, you'd have to work hard to lose a trailer down that culvert. Asleep at the wheel maybe, he came back to himself.

It's all coming home to roost, finally, I thought to myself. I returned to the table and said, for no particular reason: I love you a lot, Pete. Thanks, Mum, did Uncle Billy say where Chris and Dad are? Is he going to find them? What's happening? Then he added, warily, I heard a wildcat screeching outside, Mum, and I'm glad Dad's not here just *now* because he'd go out and shoot it. But the cat will be far away in a few minutes—I hope Dad and Peter don't come back till then.

Mack's wife phoned me after about one painful hour later, in that frosty way she had. She'd found religion a few years earlier, and now, rather than just bragging about how much she and Mack owned, she bragged about the power and quality of her God. It must have taken a lot to call—she really knew how to hate. Mack's down there helping Billy helping your son helping your husband. It all dripped off her tongue. Seems like the loader turned over in the culvert. Your son . . . Chris . . . told me . . . I went down to see if they wanted something to eat, which they did (I felt the sting in this—she clearly meant I hadn't provided adequately for my boys) . . . and was chatting with Chris, who said he *told* his Dad *not* to take the loader down the culvert any further at the angle he was on because the thing would overturn. Your husband, *typically,* wouldn't listen. *Slap, slap!* Nothing worse than being told what you know. Especially when it's yours and no one else's to really know. Don't worry, he's not hurt, she added as an afterthought or something I didn't quite get. Anyway . . . your boys should be home in an hour or two, and will be wanting a big feed, I'd guess. I'd guess too, I'd said, breaking my silence.

Truth is, though we've stuck together over the years, I would have left Bob for Billy if it weren't for the kids. And all the goings-on between the football team and Mack's wife that no one mentions these days—well, I've never discussed that with anyone but Billy. I believe Billy when he said he had nothing to do with it and went home. I believe Billy. But I believe Bob as well—he's no liar—and maybe that's why I've never confronted him with it. Why I can't ask him . . .

And with that I hastened to Peter in his bedroom, and told him all was okay—that Chris and his Dad would be home a bit later, and he could go to sleep and not have to worry, and please not to spend all night up talking with Chris when he comes in to sleep, because Chris's been working hard helping Dad and will need to get his sleep to make it to school tomorrow. He'll have good news to tell his class, Peter said in his inimitable way, and I hugged him with one arm while leaning across his bed to close a crack in the curtains that was letting in the moonlight again, steadily gaining strength outside, impossible to cut entirely out of the picture.

the pact

★ Southern Cross

They live a long way out. Isolated. Few neighbors. Few cars ever passing the front gate, which, though the property is large, is not far from the house. A few hundred meters at most.

She is alone because her husband is up on the mines. Their first season on the place didn't bring a wheat check. That augured well!—they tried to laugh it off after drinking too much. That was their nature, what they liked about each other. They'd both been farm kids whose parents had sold up during hard times in the early eighties. They knew it was foolish buying out on the very edge of the growing zone (or rather, on the edge of the arid zone), but the risk seemed worth it.

They were desperate to get out of the city. To go home. But Lucy Downs—both of their mothers had been called Lucy— was the best they could afford. Two thousand hectares of dust and patches of thinned gimlet and salmon-gum woodlands thick with wild goats. They laughed at the "Downs" bit, as the dust rolled in waves back and forth over the spread. But it was a sign of optimism. After all, it was hard to tell if they were actually in the wheatbelt or the goldfields. There was always hope of the plough unearthing a nugget!

She hears a vehicle coming down the dirt driveway, and freezes. She loves the aloneness so much that an unexpected presence is more than a fright; it alters her concept of reality. Assuming a threat, she goes to the pantry and takes out the loaded rifle. She walks carefully to the front kitchen window, eases the half-curtain back, and sees a middle-aged man in greasies and akubra getting out of a Toyota. His red cloud kelpies are on the back tray, chained to the cabin, barking excitedly.

Shut up, boys! the man says to the dogs. He has a thick accent. Maybe German, she thinks. But if so, it was a long while back. It is an ocker-German-English accent.

She leans the rifle against the wall near the doorframe, and opens the door, carefully and silently snibbing the flyscreen. Heat tumbles into the cool house. With her rough "stranger greeting" voice, she speaks through the wire.

Gidday, she says. Can I help you?

Gidday, he says. Yeah, lady. I mean, we can help each other.

She feels the pull of the rifle, but ignores it. Confident as anything, she says, I don't get ya.

Should say who I am, he says. I own Eagle View about twenty k's down the road. Few places between us, but out here we still call each other neighbors if we're on the same stretch of nothing to nowhere! He coughs a tobacco laugh.

Right, she says. Uncertain. The dogs are shaking with excitement and half choking themselves trying to jump down into the dust, into the traces of sheep shit.

Anyways, you've got caltrop up along the road round your front gate. Saw the yellow flowers through the gravel dust. Can't miss those little bastards.

No, she says flatly.

You haven't been here long. You know what caltrop looks like?

It was a rhetorical question. Not really sarcastic, more neighborly mixed with blokey condescension. She forgets about the rifle. Women are not a big part of this man's life. Probably a bachelor farmer.

Yeah, mate, grew up on a farm.

Hmmm, well, he says. Guess they've just flowered and you missed them driving out in the dust. It was that storm we had a few weeks ago that brought 'em up. Not much rain—barely filled half a rung of my big tank. But enough to stir the caltrop. Little bastards—spikes made in hell.

Yeah, their name comes from a kind of antipersonnel weapon.

He looks at her in disbelief. A mouthy woman, he might be thinking. But he kicks at the dirt and says, I wouldn't know about that, but they're worse than damned double gees. And poison doesn't seem to work. Have to get out there and pull 'em out. And walk around in a pair of thongs to collect the jacks. We've got a pact on this road to alert each other if we see any growing along the roadsides. We've managed to keep them off the properties pretty well, but they're always popping up on the verge and down the tracks, bloody cars and trucks carting them in from all parts on their tires. Sometimes it's just a bloody mystery how they get there.

Okay, mate. Wouldn't want them over our two thousand hectares. Would have a bloody sore back and go broke buying thongs.

He half-laughs, hacks, spits, excuses himself, tells his dogs to shut up, and says, Well, have a nice day. Oh, the name is Rilke, and you'll find me in the book.

She laughs, Like the poet!

What?

Oh, nothin'. Rilke—I'll remember it. I'm Desirée Cramer and my husband is Tony.

Yeah, yeah. I know, I know who you are, he says.

She baulks at that, but ticking it over, knows she shouldn't be surprised. Makes sense. Why wouldn't he? His neighbors would be told by their neighbors, who are her neighbors. Bush telegraph. Low population area. To sign off, she says, And don't worry, we'll uphold the *pact*.

Yeah, the pact, he says. The pact is *important* around here.

He stares hard in through the flyscreen, heavy red face glowering with thousands of midday suns. It's hot, and he looks hot. His eyes, deeply recessed, tell her nothing except that it's flaming hot. They are lakes of sweat threatening to burst their banks. The eyeballs are reflections of strange parallel suns. He pulls them back down further into the molten realm of his head, breaks the stare, then turns back to his vehicle, giving both kelpies a rub on the head before he gets in and drives off.

It is mid-February: the blowtorch days of summer. The last thing she feels like is going out and pulling caltrop. She wonders why she hadn't at least offered Rilke a cold drink. It hadn't crossed her mind. And thinking over it, she doubted she would have even opened the door. No reason, *really*. But offering a drink is just manners.

She feels the pressure to get the job done, compelled to deal with it immediately. She wants it out of her hair. The caltrop's presence makes her skin crawl.

Putting on a hat, she steps out of the cool of the house. Sweat instantly starts running and pooling under her thin cotton shirt. She steps inside again, slips off her bra, rebuttons her shirt, and goes back out.

She takes gloves, shovel, weeding fork, and bucket from the engine shed, and walks up the drive. She regrets not driving her air-conditioned SUV those few hundred meters.

True: around the front gate and for about three meters either side are thick infestations of caltrop. Burrs have already appeared on the long tendrils feeding out from their drought-defying taproots. It is a tangle, a Gordian knot. She gets to work, straight in. Burrs leap up and savage her fingers through the cotton gloves, and she feels herself burning on every exposed part, even through the fabric of her shirt. Sweat torments her breasts, forming humidicribs against her ribcage. She shifts, bunches and lifts her breasts every now and again, to mop up the sweat with her shirt.

It is by chance she notices Rilke's Toyota deep in the scrub opposite. The dogs are silent. He is inside the cab, watching. She can tell, though she can't see clearly. Why haven't the dogs barked? She wants to leave the work and go straight back inside the house. The cool house with good locks on the door, a telephone and a rifle. *Ridiculous* and dangerous to be working out in the heat like this.

But she persists, and doesn't look back towards Rilke, his silent dogs and silent vehicle. She doubles her efforts. Blood is soaking the gloves. Her breasts are annoying her—she no longer enjoys the brief moments when they hang free under the shirt, searching for a draft and nothingness. She crouches so contact is permanent. She is dehydrated. Nothing to drink. That was foolish too. And unlike her.

She is almost finished, on her last legs. Then the dogs bark, the Toyota starts up. She wants to run, but her knees have stopped working. She's trapped in a crouching position. By the time she forces herself up, the Toyota is alongside her and she's shrouded in dust.

Your old man should be doing this job, says Rilke, deep eyes through the open Toyota window, following it with, Shut up! to the dogs, who are growing frenzied again, their eyes rolling.

She almost says, He's not here. But she catches herself in time. Her body is hell.

You look like you've got sunstroke, he says.

I'm right. Just need to get a drink.

Your husband should have thought about things before he took on a place like this. We only count on one season in every three paying out.

We took it on together, she says.

Up on the mines like the rest of them, no doubt, he says, knowing exactly what's what.

She ignores him. Thanks for letting me know about the caltrop. Got some things to get sorted. See ya later, Mr. Rilke.

And then the door of the Toyota swings open and Rilke's heavy body half-falls out, almost on top of her.

She spills onto the ground. Her breasts move heavily under her shirt. She is swimming under the sun, the dead dry world around her.

He reaches down and grabs her arm, hauling her up. Sorry, Miss—I stuffed me hip up a few years ago on the bloody combine. Happens when I get out of the vehicle sometimes. Lose me balance.

She has wrenched her arm away and looks towards the house. She refuses to be frightened. She considers running, wondering if two kelpies would be enough to trip her up if they were released, but then thinks how much she loves kelpies. He reaches into the cab and hands her his insulated drink bottle.

Nice cool water, he says. Drink.

She grabs the bottle. Water spills over her burnt face and down her chin. She jerks her face forward to prevent it wetting her shirt, and reddens beneath her sunburn. As she clips the lid closed she sees her shirt is entirely transparent with sweat anyway. Part of her dies, and the fear that she doesn't recognize as fear goes as well. She is numb.

She stands up straight and looks Rilke deep, deep in the eye. She says, Sorry, I should have offered you a drink when you came to tell me about the caltrop.

That's okay, he says. It takes a while for new ones to *understand* the pact—its . . . complexities.

Well, I've upheld the pact, she says quickly.

Yes, yes you have.

And with that, he takes his bottle and slides awkwardly back into the cab. He tells his kelpies, who are sitting silent now, pressing against the cab to get a bit of shade, to shut up again, and drives off, this time down the road further and further, until the dust of his wheels is lost with the mirage and delusion made by the sun, still hot as hell as it lowers slowly in the sky.

the porch

★ Wongan Hills

It'd be safe to say that he's been sitting on that porch
for a good portion of thirty years, sitting there in a blue singlet
and greasies whatever the weather. He retired eight years ago,
and since then his time spent on the porch has increased. Maybe
80 percent of his waking life. Back when he was a shearer,
he'd get home and sort out his grinding straight away, have a
shower, make his tea, then settle out on the porch for three or so
hours drinking beer. If mates came around, they squeezed extra
chairs onto the porch, sat on the wooden steps, or just inside
through the flywire door, which opened straight into the lounge,
which was convenient because he could look sidewise from his
perch on the porch (his chair always faced out to the road) and
catch graph-paper versions of the footy or cricket.

The blokes on the shearing team hadn't liked it being called
a "porch," thinking it sounded vaguely ethnic and poofy, but
he said it was too small to be called a verandah—no more
than eight foot by eight foot, and stuck on the front of the
weatherboard house like an afterthought, the roof just enough to
keep the weather off, though in winter the rain blew in almost

as far as his chair against the wall. And anyway, he told the younger shearers again and again, "verandah" is a word from India—it's not even *Australian!* They never believed him, thinking it dinky di, refusing even to look it up to confirm or deny.

After he retired, only one other shearer (also retired) kept regularly visiting him. It was as if he'd never been part of a social order. Gone and forgotten. But by way of compo that one friend came most days and sat for a few hours drinking tinnies of Swan lager.

People in town had given up wondering why he sat on the porch so much. It was impossible to prise him from it unless by something already written into the fabric of his life. His friend, to whom he never referred to by name, had learnt long back, in fact, early in their shearing days, not to ask him why he just sat there. And drank. And waved to passersby.

Drink was actually the answer most wonderers resorted to: the obsessive, compulsive regularity of the alcoholic, safe in his patterns. The porch dweller chatted with his mate about the footy and the cricket and the old days and even the news at times. He wasn't really that moribund.

His friend did, however, have his suspicions. He had a hunch. And in some ways it involved him, and maybe that's why he stuck to his mate, attending the porch throne, drinking with the Lord of the Porch, and going nowhere fast.

And as they sat there one afternoon, drinking, looking out at the scant traffic on the road heading north out of town, and thinking, really, that the dry grass along the front should have been cut back before it got too hot to do so, the friend decided that he alone knew the truth, and it was time to stop beating around the bush in his own head, but also to confront his friend as he sat there, immovable on his chair on the porch.

The sky is really blue today, said the friend.

Yes, it comes with the bloody heat. There was a ring around the moon last night—gunna be a storm this evening.

You wouldn't think it. Not a cloud to be seen.

Nope, but as you know, it brews fast here. It'll start coming in around there. Mark my words.

His friend thought best to come right out with it. So he did: You know that time we met and did the run on Barry's team down around Katanning?

Yep, sure do. Five months it was. A good run. I made a packet. Helped go towards a deposit on this place. Thirty-one years, four months, and three days ago—when we first met.

His friend baulked and looked across at his mate. Gee, that's weird, how did you know that?

I know a lot of things. You'd know that if you took any real interest in me.

Hurt, his friend dropped his head and stared at a patch on his knee. Though sitting on a chair the same height as the porch dweller's, he felt so much lower, as if he was being looked down upon from a vast height. The friend listened to the crows carrying on in the jacaranda and thought he'd be damned if he went any further with his notion to confront.

But his mate had felt a pang of guilt for having a go at his friend like that. He knew he'd stepped over an unspoken boundary—insulted his guest, been a poor host. Sorry . . . just feeling off-color today. Always get like that when a storm is due, he added.

Confused, his friend spoke before thinking: At the end of the run we had a "cut out" at Hodge's farm and then went on to the pub. You were drinking with that good-lookin' rouseabout—the one with really long black hair wound up like a pyramid—and didn't go back to the quarters afterwards. You bunked down at the pub that night with her?

No reply, and nothing was said for a good half-hour, then the porch-dwelling mate replied, Yes, why bring it up now? You've never said anything about it before. Were you sweet on 'er as well?

A bit, but that doesn't matter. It's just that I—well no one I know even—ever heard of her after she—you—checked out of the pub. She told the barmaid she was heading north. Then that was it. The boss tried to contact her again 'cause she was such a good worker, but it was like she'd dropped off the planet.

Nah, she never dropped off the planet. She came here with me. I mean to this town. I was renting a place on the main street. When I bought this house she stayed for a couple of months. Then one day she walked out the door, stuck her finger out, and hitched north. Far north, she said she was going. Never heard from her again. That's what happens when you go up there. Nothing unusual about it.

Both men drank another couple of cans before the Lord of the Porch, high in his chair—*no,* higher than *ever* before in his chair—said, She loved this porch. Would sit right here where I am sitting drinking beers real slow, saying it was great watching the world slowly go by, slowly—there was even less traffic then. She was hot, as the learner-shearers would say. And smart. And she drank heaps without losing it. But she couldn't settle, and had a roving eye. Got to me that did, every now and again. Gotta admit, it got to me. Nice to feel special, unique, you know.

The friend noticed something in his mate's tone as this "confession" (was it a "confession"?) tumbled out. He wasn't sure why he asked, But you never took it out on her? I mean, you didn't give her a hiding or nothing because you were pissed off with her "roving eye"? 'Cause that wouldn't be right—I couldn't condone that, mate.

The porch dweller erupted. He leapt from his chair and hurled his seat onto the front steps. He kicked at his friend, and for the first time in decades, the friend heard his mate yell, Fuck off! Beer spilled everywhere. But the strangest thing was the mate started to cry, and slid down the weatherboards onto the deck of the porch, starting to mimic a young woman's voice, as if he was possessed, like something out of *The Exorcist*: You're smothering me, you're pinning me down, you're spinning me out! I didn't sign up for this. I am not your wife, mate, and you're an old bastard anyway. Best thing about you is your porch. This wonderful fucking porch where I can watch the world go by, go places north, go far, far away, never to be heard of again.

embarrassed

★ Dowerin region

The EK Holden first appeared on the Australian car scene—on the road—in 1961. In essence, it was a rehashed FB Holden with less silver trim. Both the FB and EK looked like sea beasts that had emerged from the great oceans that hem Australia in and hold it in place. It is said that the tail fins and the lines of these models were a nod to fifties America, but looking back, I think they were really an expression of the tension between inland and coastal Australia. I don't really know how to express this, but along with whales and sharks, the design of these cars brought to mind dead kangaroos on the side of the road, in all their traumatic and hideous beauty. Many have described the body shape of the FB and EK models as soothing and relaxing, but from an early age I found them a contradiction. They didn't fit anywhere in the world as I wanted it to be, and I didn't fit the world they came out of.

When I was twelve years old, our EK was fourteen years old. And though it had been kept in pristine condition, and though nowadays it would be a collector's item worth a mint, it was, back then in the mid-seventies, a sign of consumer failure to the kids at school, a reason for shame. It was plain "old." Not to replace old items, especially cars, was a sign of being "poor." What the rest of my family affectionately called "Old Jenny"— including my siblings, which I thought anomalous and weird— my schoolyard peers called "that old bomb."

Without going into the gory details, I will say bluntly that I was embarrassed to be seen riding in Old Jenny, by my enemies and mates alike. If Mum drove past the school in Old Jenny, I would shrink down on the bench seat—bench seats in an age when bucket seats in the front were becoming standard—shrink right down below the window. I took to walking to school in blasting rain or searing heat, even when my brothers and sisters got a lift. Mum just smiled and said, It's up to you, dear. Thirty years later I know what that smile meant.

School life is about being a new kid, or about how you react to new kids coming into *your* school. I've both experiences in my life story, but this particular story is about a new kid arriving on my block. Not really *my* block, as he moved into the wealthy enclave of town, whereas we lived "on the other side of the railroad tracks," quite literally.

It was—it *is*—a smallish rural town a couple of hours' drive from the city. It's mainly a farming center, but there is also a quarry, and back then a small open-cut ore operation was running some distance away as well. And companies were constantly exploring for new deposits of whatever.

Among those living in town, the wealthy tended to be retirees from the big farms that had been handed on to first sons, owners of the main-street businesses, the bank manager and family, the doctor and family, shire president and family, and the hierarchy of the mining operations. The new kid's father was a geologist from America! What's more, his parents had imported their fancy mile-long station wagon with false wood-grain paneling and tail fins (not, to be truthful, dissimilar in shape to Old Jenny's tail fins—just bigger and better).

We couldn't believe this new kid's name was Hank Jr. He told us the "Jr." was because his father was also Hank—Hank Sr. We would have hated him there and then had he not been the possessor of the latest yo-yo . . . and the newest pogo stick . . . and a space hopper . . . and fads and games that hadn't even arrived in Australia yet. Everybody wanted to be his friend, despite the fact he had ginger hair, which in our school was worth at least a regular corked leg or thump in the arm.

I was unsure of him in the beginning—or *from* the beginning? The latter suggests a setup, a payoff that might not really come. But I am not trying to deliver anything in particular here. Suffice it to say that Hank Jr. and I did hook up eventually, discovering that we had a love of rock hounding in common. Not surprising for him to be a rock hound, given his dad's profession, but maybe it was for me to be so dedicated. But I was a collector of many things—stamps, coins, shells, even old cigarette cards. I even had a lump of raw blue asbestos rock on my bedhead, which will probably pay off wonderfully some day not far in the future. And I had a magnificent display box my grandfather made for holding "rough rocks" in larger compartments, with small "subcompartments" for polished samples of the same rocks—for the gemstones. I accumulated my rock collection by finding rocks "in the field," swapping rocks (not often), and picking up pieces, especially gems, when we visited city weekend markets. There are always rock and gem tables at these markets. Occasionally I received bits and pieces for birthday and Christmas presents, along with other collectables. I considered myself an "easy-to-buy-for" kid and always had a list of "needs" pinned to my bedroom door for anyone to consult, should they be interested in gifting me something I really required. For collectors are people who REALLY need.

What I really needed above all other *reallies*, what every rock hound with vision craves, was a rock tumbler. A machine that polishes rocks into those smooth gems we all so admire, and project romance and spirituality through. Rock tumblers are essentially a revolving barrel with abrasive sands of differing coarsenesses, plus a cycle of "washing." You break off chunks at a roughly desired size and let the tumbler do the work. It takes weeks! I had tried to make a tumbler out of a tin can and an old electric motor, but it failed dismally.

Hank Jr., of course, had a rock tumbler, and when he heard that I collected rocks, he told me in his long, drawn-out accent that he had the best "amateur" tumbler on the American market. His father had adapted it to fit Australian electrical outlets. Hank Jr. told me this as a kind of triumph, which I could actually respect because it showed he was serious about all things rocks and gems. His father being a geologist was a secondary consideration—my issue was one of collectables and collectability.

When Hank witnessed the power he instantly acquired over me, he hung me out to dry. No invitation back to his house to see the tumbler was forthcoming. I tried taking rare rocks to school with the offer of sharing them if he'd let me participate in their polishing. It takes weeks, he said. Weeks. He watched my face closely as he repeated himself. But I could help put them in and come over to help with each stage . . . to check on their progress, I semi-pleaded. You could, he replied enigmatically, without furthering the offer.

And so it dragged on for ages and ages. But as winter came, and playing outside became less inviting, Hank Jr. began to grow bored with the social vagaries of our small rural "paradise." There were only three television stations broadcasting from the city, and only two of those could be picked up in town without a booster; even with a booster, the third was pretty snowy. Hank's many other friends lacked imagination—a game of Monopoly or Squatter (which had intrigued him so much that he bought a set for himself with his generous "allowance" and sent another set home to the States for a favorite cousin . . . "This is what the children of sheep-farmers play down here," he wrote in his card). What was more frustrating than his new friends' limited imaginations was that even the wealthier among them had the atrocious habit of breaking many of his expensive and exotic toys.

In fact, it bemused me that Hank Jr. was holding off or holding out on me . . . I mean, I *had* imagination in buckets, and I was every bit as serious about my possessions as he was, and would no sooner break something than, well, fly to the moon! Mind you, like Hank, I had every intention of actually flying to the moon as soon as I was old enough to join the space program. Hank told the class at news time one day that his father would "pave the way" for him to become an astronaut, and we all believed him. Why not?

I will say, without false modesty, that even back then I understood why he wouldn't invite me over. It would be like a frightening encounter with a mirror image of himself, or maybe a reverse image. An opposite. Part of the binary he imagined constituted the universe of himself. What would be left for him to do in our small town once he'd harnessed the energy and interest that was me? He would be more bored than he already was. And those rare local rocks he searched out on weekends with his father, hammer in hand, still eluded him . . . rocks that I possessed, that came with a life of scouring way out past the district, of having family who knew the hidden places, who listened to the stories and passed them on. Hank Jr. had actually lowered his guard early on in the piece, and snuffled around my knowledge—so, where do the a-ite rocks come from? he'd asked, pretending not to *really* care. Ha! And he'd continued, There must be a ledge, a seam somewhere in those eroded ranges south from here. Volcanic, you know. Extinct millions of years. Ancient. Yes, I know, I said, and kept my knowledge close to my chest.

It wasn't a momentous day when it came. Just a run-of-the-mill, drab winter school day when we stayed inside to eat our lunch. Or rather, "inside" under the school verandahs, crammed together along the bench seats outside the classrooms. Not truly inside—we were never allowed in the classrooms during breaks, no matter the weather conditions. The rain was blowing hard into our ankles, and it was really unpleasant. Hank sprang himself from his cluster of mates and squeezed in next to me. How are you going? he asked, in his newly acquired and ironically enforced semi-ocker accent. Fine, I said, giving nothing away.

Want to see my rock tumbler after school?

That caught me by surprise. Have to be tomorrow, I shot back rapidly. I didn't say any more. I wanted to go that day, but knew I couldn't. Mum would be angry if I just wandered off without warning after school. In this weather, what's more. She'd be waiting anxiously for me to come in, having already picked up my siblings ages before in Old Jenny, and been home a good while making pikelets. But it worked out well because my short sharp response put him on the back foot, even deflated him a little. Er, good, he replied after a while. Tomorrow. Bring your special rocks from the range. Okay.

Mum said fine and mentioned she'd pick me up from Hank's house in Old Jenny. She knew where the house was because everyone knew where everyone else's house was in our town. And though I knew he must know about Old Jenny— everyone knew Old Jenny, the "Old Bomb"—I wasn't going to give him an excuse to get started on me. It was about standing my ground, refusing to be dragged into the shame of the Old Bomb, refusing to be embarrassed.

I was my own person. I couldn't be blamed for my little brother Pete's annoying habit of chewing his pencils, or my sister Pauline's warts, or any of their other weaknesses and foibles. I was a strong individual and was defined by my own choices and actions. Annoyingly, Mum used to tell my grandparents that I was "proud," while I was standing right there! My father would say that I was "a little shit at times," but he also mysteriously called me a "chip off the old block" as he gave me a clip around the ear. But then Dad drove our real car, the family station wagon. It was a 1971 Holden, and I was happy to be seen in that, though not in the very back where the luggage, dogs, and littlies were kept or hung out.

No, Mum, thanks. I'll walk home. She just smiled at me. It would have bothered me once, that smile, but I was used to it by then and she was used to giving it. She never drove the wagon, only Old Jenny. She glowed when she drove her. Glowed like golden syrup.

Walking into Hank's house, after scrupulously wiping our shoes, was like walking into a palace. I'd been in the house before when it was owned by the Larkin family, but Hank's family had almost rebuilt it inside. Somehow, they'd sunk the lounge room. They must have excavated it, I told myself. I couldn't work out how they'd done it—unless it had always been that way and I'd taken no notice before, because the Larkins were boring people not worth taking notice of. There was thick white shag pile carpet on the floor, and pictures of jet fighters on the wall. Dad was a pilot in the U.S. Air Force before he became a geologist, Hank Jr. assured me. I was given a guided tour of the "property." More objects than I'd ever seen in one place. There was an exercise bike—a first for me. And Hank's ginger-haired mother gave us *cookies and milk* like in the Disney films. It was weird.

Where are the rocks? Hank asked. I pulled them out of my schoolbag. Let's go to work, he said.

It was an interesting process, but though I gladly paid my dues by gifting him a rare chunk of local rock, which he confirmed would polish up into a magnificent gem—and though I would receive in turn a gem polished from the other sample I took along—it was an underwhelming experience when all was said and done. Not in itself, I should say; at least not in terms of the rock tumbler. That met all my expectations—a top-of-the-list want—I'd go to work for my father during the school holidays to earn enough to buy my own. Case closed. Rather, the problem came with discovering what Hank Jr. was actually up to.

And it was appallingly simple and complex at once. It wasn't just one horror but two combined. I'd thought he was odd but never really twigged how odd one boy can be. I wanted to put it down to his being American, but I was too in love with all things American to do that. The idea of America was the sustenance I fed on to keep me alive in my small-town West Australian isolation. I wanted to blame his ginger hair, as plenty do around here, but my uncle was the toughest and most sensible man in the district and he wasn't nicknamed Blue for nothing. Whatever I thought, I wasn't about to open that can of worms. Nup, it had me stumped.

So what was he about? You won't believe it. It's embarrassing even to mention it, to give it the time of day. Shame in a rock hound—a blight on the art of collecting. Stay focused, get what you're aiming for no matter what . . . but the whole thing was confused in Hank Jr.'s single-mindedness. Your sister, he said. My sister? Pauline? A year younger than me. Than Hank. She's got warts, you know, I said. She's disgusting— and really boring, I added. Nup. He said it again. Your sister. What do you want her for? You gunna offer me your rock tumbler for her to be gift wrapped and sent to America? I couldn't help myself: I was flummoxed. Flummoxed! I'd always wanted to use that word. Then Hank Jr. suddenly changed tack. I want to ride in the back of that neat old car you've got. My dad says it's an "EK," an Aussie Classic. He does, does he? I said. I was so embarrassed now that I was beyond embarrassment. It's an Old Bomb! I shouted. No, it's in excellent condition, my dad says. He says it's in "mint condition."

For the first time in my life I didn't know what to think or say. Gee, you're a weirdo, I said at last. I'll be heading home now. You're really embarrassing, I said, walking out the door into the rain, already setting my mind firmly on the long trek home, and on how many hours I'd have to work to get myself a rock tumbler. It did cross my mind that I was signing off on both pieces of rock in the tumbler—it would be weeks before they were polished, weeks—but I didn't really mind. I had other rocks, and in a way Hank Jr. had helped my resolve, and resolve is the golden mean for any collector.

baby

★ Goomalling

I'd just come in from ploughing when I heard crying. A baby, crying. I kicked my boots off at the back door and followed the cries through to the bedroom, where I saw Margaret on the bed, leaning against the bedhead, bottle-feeding a baby cradled in her arm.

There, there, baby . . . she was saying. She didn't even notice me, which is something, given she calls me a clodhopper and the noisiest man she's ever known!

Margaret, what's going on?

She looked up at me briefly, then returned her gaze to baby, which was doing its best not to get the teat in its mouth.

Whose baby is it, Margaret?

Still not looking at me: It's mine, Alf. It's mine.

Margaret! Margaret, please tell me where the baby came from.

Those dreadful women, she spat, making baby cry all the more. I saved him from them. It's a boy child. What business have they got raising a boy child!

Lucy and Anna had arrived with baby at the vestry before anyone else to discuss the christening. The minister welcomed them in, and his wife offered them tea and cake. Ten minutes later the other women—the women on the parish committee—arrived as a group, or as a "flock," as they would joke. The minister always remarked on how in tune with each other these women were, though it was not so surprising given they'd been born and raised in the town together.

The weather was foul, but this made all cheerful as it'd been a late start to the season. Most of the husbands had been dry-seeding up until now. Margaret was first to comment, shifting uneasily in her seat but still carrying over the good humor of meeting with her old friends outside the vestry. Well, Alf got it just right this year. He's ploughing now, and if it doesn't get boggy, he'll be seeding by the weekend, and we've got rain predicted for weeks after that. We might not have the big fancy air-seeders you've all got, but we don't have so many overheads. The others nodded in agreement because they especially liked Margaret. Level-headed, generous, and polite, she was a pillar of the church community.

Anna was looking intently at the baby in its capsule. She clearly doted on it. The other ladies, apart from Margaret, gathered around and made cooing noises and said all the right things. The minister asked Lucy how it was going out at their place. I'm only putting a hundred acres in this year—just hay for the horses. I will start ploughing tomorrow. Good, good, people said, tuning into the conversation while maintaining attention on the baby.

The minister continued: Now, girls (as he called Lucy and Anna together), what is baby's name? Jordan, they both said as one. The women, except Margaret, all approved.

Margaret couldn't contain herself for long. Who chose the name? she asked. It sounded blunt in a soft place.

Anna was in such a good mood she almost sang her answer: We both did.

That's nice, said Margaret. She tapped her foot and looked out through the feature window. The vestry was such a lovely house, built in the mid-nineteenth century, separated from the church by a creek straddled by a small English-style bridge. Alf once asked her what she meant by an "English-style bridge," as she was fond of describing it that way for potential visitors to the town, to which she would reply, "It just feels English . . ." Through the window she could see the bridge and the old church beyond it. Weeping willows languidly swept the banks of the creek in the wind, and oak trees guarded the entrance to the church. There were still a few native trees about—old flooded gums and wandoos—but most of the trees had been brought from the Old Country long ago. She thoroughly approved of the "Anglican species" of trees. That's nice, she repeated, but I was wondering if the f-a-t-h-e-r had an opinion about the name?

Margaret knew what she was doing. She'd planned it for days. She was sick of this nonsense about maintaining a respectful silence when it came to the "girls." Land's sake! everybody knew they were lesbians. Margaret thought it disgusting. And, what's more, she wanted to know what right Anna had going and getting pregnant if they were such a loving lesbian couple. She was at Alf about it constantly, but he said he didn't want to know. He'd just say, Well, that Lucy can handle a header as well as Geoff, myself, or Jock.

It seemed strange to Margaret—no, more than that . . . it seemed as if the world had been turned upside down when no one—*no one*—reacted. They just kept chatting and cooing, and Lucy started a conversation with the minister about breeding alpacas, one of his special interests.

Margaret exclaimed, And does anyone know who the father is?

Anna looked up, smiled at Margaret through the crowd of women, and said, The donor is anonymous. I was artificially inseminated.

Under normal circumstances, Margaret would have behaved like the other women (and minister) and filtered out the facts she didn't want to know. Politeness would have won out, and harmony would have been maintained. But something had shifted in Margaret the moment she heard about the christening-to-be. And when the rain came, and Alf was out the door to get the ground ready for the wheat, she could contain herself no longer. She rang her son in America. A college professor now, who just laughed and told her to relax and get *with it.* The world has changed for the better, Mum. She rang her daughter, a farmer's wife on a big spread down south. Mum, don't get so worked up about it. Even if it's not our way, live and let live. Margaret wasn't just upset. She was incensed. She even pulled her favorite staghorn off the verandah post and dashed it to the ground.

Margaret, how did you get the baby?! Where did you get it from? Alf was beside himself now—fear and anger and pity rolled into one. She ignored him, so he went into the hallway to the telephone. He paused for a minute as the baby stopped crying—it had obviously taken the teat. Looking down the hall and into the kitchen, he saw new baby bottles on the sink. He noticed other baby stuff he hadn't seen when he walked in. He'd been tired. On the tractor for fifteen hours. His body was buzzing with it. He could barely think straight. He walked down the corridor in the other direction and took a left at the intersecting corridor, to the kids' old bedrooms. His son's was as it always was. His daughter's was done up with a cot and change table and everything else. All brand new. Even in his astonishment and distress, he couldn't help thinking what it had all cost! And how long it had been planned for. He went back to the phone and dialed the family doctor at home. He didn't know what else to do. No answer. He dialed Margaret's best friend, June: no answer. He dialed the minister, who was home, and when he heard what Alf had to say he let out a scream, a real scream, and dropped the phone.

Alf spoke to Lucy out front while Anna went inside to see the baby, to see Margaret. Shouldn't we go in as well? said Alf. No, said Lucy, Anna wants to deal with it herself. Thanks for not calling the police, said Alf. He stared out into the misty rain, out over the bare paddocks, not knowing what else to say. He felt bad, real bad. He was filthy and wanted a shower but knew it wasn't the right thing to be thinking. The inside of his head was a mess. Nothing made sense. How many acres are you seeding this year, Alf? asked Lucy. A thousand, said Alf. I'd like to put in more, but that's all I can afford to seed this year. Been hard over the last few years. But I don't need to tell you that. Same for everyone. He gently jerked his head in the direction of the house, in the direction of his and Margaret's bedroom, and said, It's taken a toll on some. You know, everyone thinks it's the blokes who suffer most, but it's not. The women take it hard as well. Real hard.

He thought about apologizing to Lucy for the obvious, but she pushed her hair back off her forehead and stamped her boot and said, Yep, it's true, and Alf was grateful that he didn't need to explain anything. A ray of sunlight broke through the clouds, and a patch of blue opened out. He stared deep into it, and beyond. I've done a lot of things wrong on this place over the years—the soil isn't so good, and if I hadn't done so much clearing as a young bloke, we wouldn't have the same salt problem we've got in the paddocks down by the creeks. I like what you and Anna have done with all those trees, with the way you handle the land. The way you *nurture* it. I am trying to put it right now. He said this stamping the ground and staring at his boots. He hadn't liked the way he'd said "nurture" . . . it sounded bitter. It *was* bitter. He kicked his doubts and frustration into the dirt and lifted his face, smiling.

Lucy replied, Yeah, it's never too late, I say. Or better late than never. We want Jordan to have something worth inheriting. There was silence, with just the trickle of rain still running off the roof into the guttering and out of the pipe from the roof into the nearby rainwater tank. It became a slow and steady plip plip plip.

When christening day came and people heard that Margaret had been named godmother, there was a ripple of surprise that grew to a flood. In the days that followed the "mishap," Alf and Margaret had felt the full weight of the town's anger. Alf wanted to say to some of his old friends, You were the first to call down the wrath of God on the girls' heads and wanted to drive them out of town. And that was long before a baby came into the picture. He couldn't understand the shift, and though their cruelty to Margaret pained him, he also took pride in the shift of attitude the town had managed, without really knowing why. That was something. And though he wasn't a superstitious man, he felt that a christening, and one which they were so blessed to be part of, was a good omen for the spring that would come, and the harvest it would bring. It had rained steadily and would keep raining. The crops would grow. And as Lucy said to him when Anna came out with the baby in her arms, Jordan means "down-flowing," and the river will run for all in the shire.

the garden

★ Goomalling

Water had to be carted over half a dozen small hills and a dozen sizeable paddocks to sustain the garden. The garden, within its crown-of-thorns fencework dug deep to keep the rabbits out, was surrounded by pasture already yellow not long after winter, and the desire lines of sheep trails, those hills, and not a single tree. An outsider seeing it distantly from the ribbon road would say, God, there's a vegetable garden out here in the middle of nowhere! An island. An oasis. A mirage?

It certainly wasn't nowhere, and Howard would be the first to tell a stranger so. It was his center, and making it lush, making it yield in extreme heat and dryness, was his pleasure, his purpose. This wasn't just a sense of beating the elements, but a satisfaction in showing such a feat was possible. And the vegetables, especially the corn, melons, and tomatoes, all keen for water, were the sweeter for it. It was the summer garden he prized, leaving the ground fallow over winter. The air above his garden buzzed with freshness and moisture, while everything beyond its shores was nearly too dry to breathe. Out there, the air was brittle.

Mostly he carted water in a tank on the back of his old tray-top utility, a slightly brackish water from a windmill-drawn bore down near the soak, which dried out in spring. But sometimes, when he was feeling particularly overwhelmed by the glory of his garden, he would fill an old firefighting water pack, hoist it on his back, and cart it three miles over the hills. That would be for the early morning or evening, when the sun was out of the way or casting long shadows, but was all the same dangerous even from where it lurked.

His family thought him barmy, but didn't say much because he still owned the farm, and they all hoped to inherit. His younger son cropped a large section, and ran sheep as well. *He* didn't say anything because he didn't consider it his business. He lived in a separate house on the property with Susan, his wife, who would say, When we have children this arrangement will have to change. It's just so weird.

She and her husband enjoyed the fruits of the garden. Neither of them bothered Howard's work there or ever went near it. But they had seen him there over the years—a glimpse from a distance, or having to find him once when a relative had passed away. Susan had said, He almost makes love to those vegetables. All those shapes and colors. The younger son replied, Fair crack of the whip, let it go! Which she did.

Howard never considered himself lonely, though he did miss *his* wife. She'd been a wonderful gardener. She'd once said to him, I'd like to cover the deserts of the world in vegetables and feed all the starving. Howard remembered this, and after she died, watering the vegetables in the kitchen garden, he had an epiphany. He would grow vegetables on the farm, where they were least likely to succeed.

Winter was the quiet time. As the crops grew around him, he tended the kitchen garden his wife had established decades earlier, but he stayed away from the paddock garden. And he stayed inside. You should get out more, Dad, said the younger son. But whenever Howard suggested helping the lad with fencing or lambing or shearing, he got the brush-off. You've worked hard all your life, Dad, now it's my turn. And we can afford to hire men when we need them. Howard spent the rest of his time inside, watching television, looking through photo albums though he hadn't taken a photo since his wife's death, and planning the summer garden. Time went neither fast nor slow in winter; it was just a blank, a hyphen linking the seasons of his remaining life together. But he didn't really dwell on it.

The elder son was jealous of the younger, and was just biding his time. District lore said the elder should inherit, and when he did, there would be a fire sale. The elder and his second wife, Lorna, visited twice a year to see how things were going. But they never visited in summer, the heat out in the central wheatbelt too much for either of them to bear. The elder son was successful in the city, and since arriving at his Church of England private school at the age of twelve, had never looked back at the country with any yearning. He was, as they say, a pillar . . . And Lorna far exceeded the social triumphs of his first wife, who had—almost shamefully—passed away with breast cancer. The elder son had considered that extremely unfortunate, damaging to his prospects. But he had picked himself up, grateful there'd been no children yet, and moved quickly on to Lorna, who bore him two sons now ensconced as boarders at the same elite school he himself had attended, even though they lived in the neighboring riverside suburb and could have been day boys.

But *that* summer the elder son and his wife did drive up, because the time had surely come when Howard was about to join Mother. They both felt death was in the air and wanted to assert their presence. It was logical; Howard was very old and didn't have much to live for. He had pined from the moment Mother had died.

And it was from the ribbon road that they caught sight of Howard. The horror. Lorna saw him first, then elder son. They didn't hesitate, but drove straight to younger son's house, pushed past him without a word to his wife, Susan. Lorna barely acknowledged her brother-in-law, but she knew Susan was probably her match.

Lorna spoke first. Susan, we have just seen Father down the paddock.

Susan saw an opening, In his silly garden? Among the melons and zucchini?

No idea, darling, it was too far to see what species of greenery. But he was in a garden surrounded by dust and he was wearing—

A bloody dress! screamed the elder son.

Susan said blithely to Lorna, whom she detested, So now you know what the whole district knows. Just be grateful you don't live with the shame.

He's sick! yelled the elder son.

He's lonely, replied the younger.

Needless to say, different as they all were and are, the family came to an agreement about Father; about Dad. The time had come. They could afford to put him in a home, and Father—Dad—wouldn't have grounds to object. They didn't make a fuss, but all walked up, took photos, and walked back. Howard hadn't even seemed to notice them, which was further evidence.

What got Howard, lying in his nursing-home room, rubbing his fingers together and sensing the skin of his tomatoes and the skin of his late wife, the texture of corn silks and the fabric of his wife's underwear, was how abundant the garden was, urging harvest. It was on the verge. They didn't even give him a chance to pick. He stared at a photo of the farm his younger son had brought in—bare fields, not a tree in sight, sheep. Thought it'd cheer you up, his son had said. The elder was busy—he and his brother weren't talking. But Lorna and Susan were getting on better these days. They'd reached a watershed, and every now and again popped in to see Dad—Father—not too often; they didn't want to seem coarse. Susan would never have used such a word before she got to know Lorna better.

What got Howard was the waste—he knew, deep down where it counts, deep like the bore water that had fed his garden, that none of the vegetables would have been harvested, none of them eaten once he'd *gone.* He listened to the waves of the air-conditioning and felt the farm's dead winds buffeting the garden. Soon the windmill would die and the deserts would grow and the peoples of the world starve.

the vacant block

★ Merridan

It was one of the larger inland wheatbelt towns, with substantial rail yards and massive wheat bins. Locals considered it the state's heartland. Kids would say, If someone drops a lit cigarette into the grid of that A-type bin, the whole town will explode.

Almost half the grain harvest of the wheatbelt came from the low-rainfall, not overly rich lands that filled out its district. The great arterial highway running from west to east serviced the town and serviced travelers driving through to the nugget of the Goldfields, Kalgoorlie. The population was about two-and-a-half thousand; just enough for a suburban infrastructure that is really rural without land. The shopping was adequate, but the three-and-a-half-hour trip to the city's big shops was always at the back of the mind, if rarely made. There was a train service a couple of times a week, which pensioners tended to patronize because they got cheap fares.

Being on the great highway meant the shops had relatively fresh produce most days, but narrowly and not imaginatively selected. Just your staples with a few exotics. It suited the town's taste, in the main. Demand followed its own logic there, but was more logical than towns off the beaten track.

Even for those living in the town itself, rather than on the outskirts or on small properties buffering the town here and there before the massive landholdings began, the ordinary house block never really felt far away from the saltlands that besieged the town's prosperity and future. Townies were almost as much part of the *land* as those who lived outside town. Maybe, in some mysterious unanswerable ways, more so.

And in *answerable* ways for those who'd had their land taken from them, who'd been forced into the municipal clutches. Non-indigenous townsfolk called them "the Blacks" or "the Abos," though some called them by their tribal names, or "Aborigines." A begrudging respect for the Blacks had crept into the wider community; some even acknowledged they were traditional owners with a long history and understanding of the place. On special formal occasions there were welcomes to country, and a few of the town's officials looked as if they actually meant it when they gave thanks to the elders. Yet although in some ways respect was coming into the town, fear and racism ran deep, as every "Black" would confirm.

Mr. Synge, a non-Black and retired businessman from the city, owned two town blocks midway between the outskirts and the main street. He'd left the city way down south, looking for investment opportunities and something equating to the country childhood he remembered with affection. He considered his blocks the civic core of the town. On one quarter-acre block he had his own house, an old asbestos job built in the early fifties, and right next door, a vacant quarter acre that he planned to sell "when the market is at its peak." This vacant block was bare, other than for wild oats and a few fruit trees down near the back fence. For his first ten years in town, Mr. Synge ran a small electrical appliances shop, which he sold at a tidy profit (as he liked to say).

It was fifteen years since he'd bought the two blocks. The vacant one was an investment for the future, though in truth, considering inflation, it hadn't appreciated enough to prompt him to sell it. The market just hadn't peaked, though he knew it would one day, and he'd "make a killing!" It was his investment for the grand European trip he intended to take with his wife in their retirement. Yet whenever they came to discuss it, they ummed and aahed, maybe not really wanting to leave the dryness, heat, familiarity.

And the vacant block was like a spare limb should he ever become incapacitated. Though his wife *had* wanted him to sell it for years, she'd given in. She liked the fruit trees—an orange, a lemon, a mandarin, two apples, and three figs—that persevered despite the lack of water. Each year when they were in flower and fruiting, she covered them with netting to keep the parrots off. She emptied her washing water over their trunks. Good for scale, and keeps them watered, she said.

With all of this in mind, you can imagine the shock when Mr. and Mrs. Synge returned from a picnic at the local Rock (wheatbelt towns have large granites they set compasses and personal magnets by), to find massive piles of tree prunings dumped in the middle of their vacant block. They could see the tire marks of a truck leading up to the piles. Mr. Synge swore so loud, neighbors down the street came out and stood on their dead lawns.

Even though there was no specific or even logical link to the graffiti that had been scrawled across the block's old super 8 fences some months before, Mr. Synge still made such a connection. The cops, scowling at each other in their deliberations, had said it was kids. Kids it might have been. But kids didn't have access to trucks, and they didn't prune trees. Lots of trees.

Mr. Synge was the *last* person to see graffiti as "work," but though it filled him with wrath, it was clear the pruning was work. Anyone willing to work, and dump the result of that work on his vacant block, was particularly malicious to his way of thinking—and with a plan. He didn't credit graffiti "tagging" (the cops' term) as having a plan, though it too was malicious, but more of the empty-headed variety rather than of the carefully executed. This was his reasoning.

Though surely these different acts of vandalism to Mr. Synge's property were connected, even if tenuously. Maybe the children of some family were graffiti "artists," and the parents were topiarists. He laughed, just a little, at this thought. Mr. Synge would leave no stone unturned in catching what he now considered was an entire family of perpetrators—young and old. By yoking the graffiti and the dumping into one incident, he felt better able to focus and catch the criminals. He had little faith in the police sorting out the problem.

But before he had a chance to pursue a line of inquiry, Mr. Synge caught a cold that quickly turned to pneumonia. This annoyed him, because it wasn't even winter. It was a serious case; the medical people said he was lucky to survive. His wife spent day and night by his bed. He told the staff at the hospital his wife was a good woman, and *they didn't make them like her any more*. The nurses thought him a card, and laughed at all his outdated jokes. They said to Mrs. Synge, That husband of yours could talk a hind leg off a horse!

When he returned home, the Synges found a package on their verandah. It was a carton of fruit. Exotic fruit—the kind grown up at Carnarvon, or even right up on the Ord River in the Kimberley. And there was a card with large-lettered spidery writing that said, We hope you are feeling better, Mr. Synge.

They were touched, but had no idea who could have done such a thing. It choked Mr. Synge up, because as a young man he'd worked up on the Ord River in the early days of the scheme. He'd been a traveling salesman, offering the new vegetable farmers electrical equipment. Are you okay, dear? asked Mrs. Synge. And Mr. Synge could convincingly reply, Will be a while before the chest feels right again.

A few days later there was a knock at the door. Mr. Synge had been on the phone to the police numerous times over the last day or two, regarding progress (or not) in capturing the offenders. He was back on the case. As he'd suspected, his absence meant the case had gone cold. No leads, and the forensic trail lost to the wind and heat.

Will you get that, dear? he yelled to his wife. I am trying to reach the sergeant again. He's always out! I think they should do a door-knock—some damned basic detective work!

A few seconds later, Mrs. Synge showed a small girl into the lounge room. Mr. Synge covered the phone's mouthpiece and said, Well now, who do we have here? You're one of the Hill kids from a few doors down?

Yes, said the girl faintly.

She's shy, said Mrs. Synge. Their children had long grown up and left home, and were living in far-off places. They had almost no contact with the very young.

What do you want, darling? asked Mrs. Synge.

To see if the old man would like anything? Mum and Auntie said they could do the shopping for you.

Mrs. Synge looked across to her husband, who had absentmindedly hung up the phone. Mrs. Synge didn't drive and was not strong, and Mr. Synge was under orders to stay home and rest. By rights he should still have been in bed. They spoke to each other in silences, before Mrs. Synge said to the girl, Please thank Mummy and Auntie, and tell them I will come and see them.

With that the girl looked relieved, and skipped off.

You could strike me down with a feather, said Mrs. Synge.

It's odd, said Mr. Synge, but he was not sure why.

He looked troubled, forgetting the investigation. The two of them said little for the rest of the day. After dinner, Mrs. Synge said, I should pop around and thank them.

Yes, yes, you should, said Mr. Synge. There was another uneasy silence. You'll be okay? said Mr. Synge.

Yes, yes, of course, said Mrs. Synge. Strange, I've never spoken with them before. Been on the street longer than we have.

Mr. Synge coughed, concentrating on the evening news. Mrs. Synge sat and stared into space.

I was a bit short with the mother, years ago. When I still had the shop. She didn't have the little one, just the older boys, and they were with her when she came in asking for her old television to be repaired, and I just said, now I can't do anything about it, lady, without even looking at it. And she just stared at me and looked angry, then started to cry, and I just went back to what I was doing, and I heard her shuffling her boys out and saying, We'll have to take it to Kal, boys.

Mrs. Synge had never heard him blurt things out that way before. He was crying. In all their years together, he'd never shed a tear over anything. She shook, worried now for his health, and thought of ringing the hospital.

Well, that's a long time ago, she reassured him.

Yes, a long time ago, he muttered.

The phone rang. Mrs. Synge picked it up and said, It's for you, darl, it's the sergeant, ringing from home. After hours! Now, that's service.

Mr. Synge rocked in his seat and said, Ask him what he wants. Just ask him for me.

Mrs. Synge nodded.

Yes, yes, yes. Aha, ah, that's it. Thank you very much, sergeant, I knew you'd get to the bottom of it. Yes, that still leaves the graffiti, but I am sure you'll solve that as well. Yes, you have your suspicions. Yes, yes, we all know who it was. You'd expect it from their kind. Aha, yes, yes. Enjoy your dinner, sergeant.

It was the shire workers, darl, dumping cuttings from the other side of town. Their excuse is that they'll collect it when they do the streets around here—you know, clipping the box trees.

Mr. Synge said, Makes about as much sense as you'd expect.

And the sergeant hasn't charged anyone yet, but he's pretty sure that it's very likely, even inevitable, that it's black kids—black *boys*—from near here who made that awful mess of our fence.

Then, in a way he hadn't done since he was a small child, Mr. Synge put his hands to his ears and repeated, over and over, I don't want to hear.

Mrs. Synge was worried. She would ring the hospital. Something was very wrong with Mr. Synge. Flustered, she said, We must protect our property, darl. That block is our dream holiday to Europe. If we put it on the market, buyers won't want to see alien words scrawled all over the place.

I don't want to hear, I don't want to hear, I don't want to hear. I'm going to call for help!

Mr. Synge snapped out of it. I'm fine. Go and see those people and say thanks. We'd be delighted to have their help.

His wife looked frightened. I'm prepared to thank them, but do we really need to ask for help?

We're not asking; they're offering.

All the same, she said, they're different from us, they're . . .

I don't want to hear, I don't want to hear, I don't want to hear!

With that, Mrs. Synge rose from her chair, went to the bathroom to tidy her hair, said good-bye to her husband, and set off for the Hills' house, only a few doors down but further than the city, further than Kalgoorlie or Carnarvon or even the Kimberley.

Yet as she knocked on their door, she thought how easy it was, *really*.

Both Mrs. Hill and Mrs. Synge studied each other carefully before saying hello across the threshold, before Mrs. Synge stepped confidently inside.

the house near
the cemetery

★ Meckering/Cunderdin

Well, I've been doctoring in this town for forty years, and I know a bit about what goes on behind the scenes. I wasn't born and bred here—I actually did my early doctoring down in Albany, and have a love of that wild coast. Like most of the older people in this town, I take my annual holidays down there, and that helps me keep a perspective on this place. Don't get me wrong, I love it here, but I've never really felt part of it. An eternal outsider. But as a doctor, I think that's an advantage—people will tell you things they wouldn't tell others. If they feel you're outside the "blood" of the place, they're less likely to gossip. From what I hear, the doctor before me, who was born and bred here, and came back much later in life to serve out his last medical years as town GP, was always suspected of betraying confidences, though in reality I'd say he never uttered a word out of place.

I hear a lot of unusual things that need to remain between me and my patients. But I will tell you a story that's not often mentioned, though it runs like a spinal cord through the psyche of the town, and is no great secret. Rather, it's just not spoken about, in the hope that shifting generations will push it aside to a minor part of the body—a nerve in a finger or a toe that might twinge every now and again but can be effectively ignored. One of the main players is dead now, and his wife is in a nursing home in Perth. The daughter lives in town still.

The old house down by the cemetery had long been vacant. It was on land belonging to Nick the Slav, as they called him, and though it wasn't right next to the cemetery, it was the closest building to the graves. Maybe a half mile away, out in the middle of a paddock. One old pepper tree in the house yard, and a well that was almost dry, but there was enough fresh water down there to get by on. The house itself was in a sorry state. The walls had been cracked open by the Meckering quake of '68, and the floors torn apart. Nick was in there at the time with his wife and daughter, and they all ran outdoors as the place began to shake and shake and buckle. When the quake stopped, they huddled together in the family station wagon, though they feared each aftershock and tremor might be the start of another big one that'd open up the ground beneath the wagon and swallow them whole. They weren't far wrong—the fault line weaves its way through the neighboring farm, and if you look down from the hill it's like a ledge that extends for miles. Before the quake, it was all flat.

Nick and his family never stayed another night there. They moved into town, and Nick ran the farm from a distance, going out every day to his sheds, which were a short way from the house but sustained little damage by comparison. The steel frame of one shed buckled a bit, but not much else.

A "clearer" in his youth—hacking out scrub and burning off thousands of acres—Nick had never forgotten the bonfires he helped feed for years. He'd said to the woman who would become his wife that the fires had looked like dying stars, or like the sun suffocating in its own smoke. She found him poetic, and didn't regret coming all the way from the Old Country to start a new life. They'd known each other in childhood, and their families had always considered they'd be married. But before they tied the knot, Nick had been living in work huts and learning the language—he wrote to her to say he had saved enough to buy a small farm on marginal land.

So they were married, and his wife was quickly pregnant, and their daughter eventually taught her mother to speak English faster and more efficiently than Nick had ever managed, though he was always something of a poet. He would often tell his daughter, as she grew up, tales of his life as a clearer. But she didn't like to hear because he became worked up, and sometimes scared her. He'd say, I cut and burnt all I could see, and further than I could see. I did it to earn enough to make my family, but the whole time I was doing it, I felt it was wrong. I watched the large animals flee as we cut the wood, I watched small animals burn in the fires, caught emerging from under the bark of trees, or having made their homes among the dead branches. I saw fledglings of parrots choke in their fallen hollows, and I heard the land weep at night. I was told by some who had known the land for much longer, who were cutting and burning the land they loved because they had no other way left to feed their own families, that bad would come of this.

But that was a long time back, and at the time of the quake their daughter was looking to move out into the world, and the couple were thinking of retiring to town anyway.

So the house was left abandoned. And even when Nick went out to work in the sheds, he ignored it. For him, it was blighted. He would never say why, but if you'd seen this man, who was known to fear nothing, shake long after the ground had finished shaking, you'd know he'd sealed a pact with his maker that if he got his family safely out of there, he'd start a new, more pious life. And, indeed, he did become a regular at church, and his daughter did marry into one of the most respected Catholic families in the district.

In time, Nick moved his sheds to another part of the property. He'd never liked working near the cemetery anyway. He donated some of his land to the town so the cemetery could expand, and, other than preserving the firebreaks, he left that part of his farm to its own devices. Jam tree and York gum saplings had sprung up all over that hundred acres, and it was slowly turning back into bush. But around the house, within the house yard, except for the pepper tree, nothing grew. Not even grass. It was as if some poison had been spread and killed off anything that might have had a chance to emerge. But there'd been no poison used there, and there was no logical explanation. Nick, however, didn't want to know and didn't want to care.

Though so much had grown back in the paddock, the view from the cemetery to the house was fairly unobscured. Inevitably, those visiting the dead, or taking their dead to rest, would look out at the house and wonder. It wasn't quite old enough to be an interesting relic, a piece of wheatbelt history, but it had been there for a good fifty years before Nick bought it, so it did have some history. A mix of wooden boards and stone, it looked Federation-era. It sparked enough interest for people to say, One day I'll go across and take a look—but not quite enough for them to remember after they'd left the cemetery. Of course it was the dead who really occupied their thoughts, as you'd expect, while they were there. Sometimes visitors would drop by this out-of-the-way place and look at names and dates on the graves, collecting, hoping for a vicarious sense of belonging, to meld their living bodies to the phantom bodies of the dead and lay a sort of claim, but few of them would have risked walking across private land to take a look at a ruined house. City folk who come out on weekend trips into the country always fear being shot by mad landowners.

One day, however, a young couple did decide to make their way over the cemetery fence, over the firebreak, and through the overgrown and neglected paddock, to the old house. They'd been in the cemetery paying their respects to a young man who'd died in a road accident. A local who had a huge funeral a couple of months earlier—a much-loved youth. This couple, Dave and Julie, who'd been distant friends of his from the city, couldn't make the funeral, but promised themselves that whenever they had the chance, they'd get out there and make it right. They managed to borrow that young man's father's car, and drove the four hours from the city without a break. Finding the town roadhouse, they fueled up, got something to eat, and got directions to the cemetery.

From the cemetery, over the wild growth, they saw the house. They were mesmerized. Julie was the driving force . . . Dave was uncertain, but agreed to climb the fence, then helped Julie over. The grass and low scrub caught in their jeans, and both received a few scratches. Wow, what a place, looks like the dead zone. They didn't hesitate to go in, and balance and teeter their way through the rooms, marveling over the damage, which they had no idea was caused by the quake.

Julie had been saving a couple of acid trips in her purse for a special occasion. Let's drop them, Dave. Let's camp out for the night. It's hot and there'll be a full moon and the skies are clear. It'd be amazing! It'd be a spinout.

Dave wasn't so sure. Okay, but let's get some water and stuff in town and come out again. They were back in an hour, making themselves comfortable as possible and waiting for the trips, which they'd just dropped, to come on.

Dave later described the way the trips came on, making them laugh uncontrollably, making them find everything "amazing." I won't trouble you with his description of their elation and trauma, but go straight to the point where a shared paranoia crept in, and they found themselves terrified. Nothing in particular happened, I say, but small things became great, and they convinced themselves the house was shaking and buckling and that they were in the middle of an earthquake. There weren't even any tremors in the region at the time—I checked.

Now, paranoia is a common thing with LSD, especially when the trips are preserved with a large dollop of strychnine. They were having a bad trip. This is part of Dave's description:

We both saw the roof melt away, and the moon burned right through us. We couldn't hide from its rays. The walls started closing in, and the bits of floor that weren't already broken and buckled started to toss us about. Retreating onto the open dirt patches where there were collapsed floorboards, we felt the earth opening up like a giant mouth, and we held on to each other knowing that we'd be going into the belly of the whale together. That was our only comfort. We could both hear singing, like the sea, and many other voices chattering away at us. Somehow we lifted ourselves out of the mouth and crawled outside the house, down the steps and onto the dead ground. The moon was still burning us, so we crawled under the great old pepper tree, the only other shelter near the house. We wrapped ourselves around its gnarled trunk and watched the dead ground melt away—we were suspended over a great cavernous pit. No longer a mouth but a pit without end, like a gigantic mine. The house and the tree and us holding the tree hanging there, suspended. And as we looked down into the pit, we saw thousands of fires. Men and women and children were feeding these fires with great trees they just plucked out of the depths. It was as if all the bush and all the forests of the world were being burnt at once. The people's expressions were clear, though they were so far below. They seemed so determined, so hardworking, so convinced they were doing the right thing. We felt for them, we really did—but as the time passed, our grip on the suspended tree weakened and we knew we'd fall and be consumed by the fires.

And that's where Dave stopped. He wouldn't tell me any more; neither would Julie. They had been found wandering on the cemetery road, babbling to themselves. Both were far from novices with drugs. Something had really spooked them. They were brought into the hospital, and I was called straight away. I gave injections of Valium. I don't think I'm breaching confidentiality to say that, since within days every detail of the story was out anyway.

Now, that might seem all there is to tell, and weird enough in itself, but the real twist is in the tail. Somehow, gossip about what had happened reached Nick and his family's ears, and in no time at all Nick, his wife and daughter were up at the hospital, demanding to talk with Dave and Julie. At first I thought it might be something to do with trespassing, but when I started defending them as curious young people, Nick waved his hand angrily and said, You think I care about that. Never. There is much more at stake here! I must see them! Wife and daughter tugged at his shirt, and he threw them a wild look and turned back to me, We must talk with them!

I pointed out that the two were very distressed and had toxins in their system (I never said what) and needed rest, but Nick insisted he could help them. I'd always liked and trusted Nick and his family, so I pacified him: I'll ask them if they're willing to talk to you. What should I say it's about? If I tell them you are the owner, they'll be worried. No, no, said Nick, just say we can tell them something that will bring them peace. I cocked an eyebrow at this, but took the message through into the bowels of our small hospital anyway.

Though it's not usual practice to put a male and a female in the same room, I had done so for fear of agitating them further with separation. They clung to each other like barnacles to a ship's hull. I put Nick's words to them; they looked across the room at each other nervously, and then just nodded "okay."

Now, Nick asked for himself and his family to be left alone with Dave and Julie, but I drew the line there. Once again, Nick tried my patience, but I insisted it couldn't happen. As a further placation, and by then I was at my limits, I politely asked the nurse who was in with the two patients to go and attend to another duty further down the corridor. I stood by the door, watching and listening—I make no apologies for that.

Nick said he and his family also "knew the house." It was *our* house, he said. I was in the house with my wife and daughter and the great earthquake tore our house open. Before it struck, the birds had gone silent and the dog howled and whined. We never saw the dog again after the quake struck. And everything about the house died. We retreated to our car and saw the earth open beneath us and we hung in the air with nothing more than the house and the pepper tree and in the distance, the cemetery. We watched the spirits lift from the graves that had been cracked open, and they flooded across the paddock and held us, kept us from falling. I felt blessed and damned at once. Blessed and damned.

And then Nick and his family turned and left the room and an unsettling calm fell across the young couple's faces.

the appointment

Kelleberrin
area

After patients have drops put in, they are placed in
a half-lit room. Gradually, pupils dilate and patients become
grateful there's only enough light to see by, and not enough
to bother their suddenly sensitized eyes. There's a window, but
it's heavily curtained, and a corona glows around the edges,
clarifying and emphasizing the frame's chipped lead paint. The
carpet is threadbare because it doesn't need to be any different,
though you can feel it through the thickest of shoes. This
surgery is in a wealthy area—an old house done up. The rest of
the building is so comfortable with wealth that it would seem
uncouth to mention the carpet in the "dark room."

There are only two patients in the room at this time. Both
roughly the same age—maybe just the other side of "pension
age"—and both slowly becoming aware of each other beyond
that *stranger in the room*. They start to chat, as people cloistered
in this room usually do.

As it happens, they turn out to be from almost neighboring
wheatbelt towns. The woman describes herself as the wife of a

farmer, and the man describes himself as a farmer with a wife. Conditions of engagement thus set, they chat about people they know in common and farms they have both visited, wondering how they can have spent a lifetime in practically the same district without knowing each other. They qualify this: I'm sure I've heard your name mentioned over the years . . . Yes, likewise . . . Maybe our rams have competed against each other at Dowerin Field Day . . . or your wife's jams have come up against mine . . . though I'm sure I'd remember, because I know the name of every second and third prize to my firsts over the years . . . and I know whose rams mine have beaten.

As their eyes widen and they can see each other more clearly in the strange light, they become even more enthusiastic. They are sitting on a wooden bench—a church pew, really—against a wall, a few feet apart. A polite, respectable distance. There is nothing else in the room. They are dressed in their city best. She is in a blue slack suit; he's in a corduroy jacket and pants. All brown, just like her husband wears. The colors are muted, but recognizable. Familiar, even in that light, with these eyes.

It was a long drive down, and someone would be driving them back, because you can't drive after eyedrops. And that brings them constantly back to their partners, just as the bench leads to talk of their local churches. When they were built. What the congregations are like. Their unknowing of each other could be explained by their churchgoing. One is Catholic and the other C of E. Discovering this, they twinge a little, but talk around their differences as if describing different instalments of the same denomination.

When they get to the topic of their respective farms, things really flow. Laughing gently, they suppose they'd better keep their voices down, as the specialist, the patient he was at present treating in the surgery, eyes already fully dilated, and those in the waiting room, will hear them through the stone walls!

He tells her how good the wheat harvest was on his property last year. No one else in the district, in fact in the whole region, pulls as many bags off an acre as we did.

With a small laugh, she begs to differ. We had the best season in the district, in fact in the whole region! They compare yields: exactly the same.

There you go! It seems even stranger they've never met. That the families aren't known to each other—aren't friends—despite the difference in religions. It's a lot more tolerant—the place, that is—these days. Lot more tolerant than during our—childhoods . . .

With their healthy wheat cheques, both families had bought a new header. Yet more in common.

The room seems to be getting brighter, but they know it just means their dilated eyes are catching more of the light that is floating around. She admires how cleanly shaven he is, and he admires how her sculpted hair sits so perfectly in place. They do not register each other's grey hair—that has long been normal.

Then comes that awkward silence. They've said what they had to say. If they'd been friends meeting in the main street of town—either of their towns—it'd be time for: Well, I've got a lot to do this morning. Moving on before doubt about the other had entered the mind. Wheatbelt towns—towns everywhere?—work like that.

But here they are *stuck* with each other for at least another ten minutes. Now she notices his annoying habit of tapping his foot. She stares at his patent leather shoes. Almost expensive-looking, but he's done a poor job polishing them. Her eyes seem to be working better than ever. She can see in the dark. He doesn't take the hint—her staring at the shoes. That's a hint.

She is sure the foot-tapping is a habit of his. A nervous reaction, she tells herself. I bet he does it all the time. If I were his wife, I'd have nipped it in the bud as soon as we'd married. She is too polite to say anything, but if they were friends she certainly would. He notices her habit of sucking her lips. Dentures, he guesses. Or just dry lips. Either way, it's irritating. I wouldn't tolerate it with my wife! He smirks.

Time slows down so that they both wonder if the drops are affecting them in an unexpected way. The seconds grind like hours. They fidget on their seats and are embarrassed, though they work hard not to show it.

One of them says, We've got a bad policeman in town . . .

That so?

Yes.

How?

It's the way he interacts with the blacks.

The Aborigines?

Yes. We've got some bad sorts in our town. You know, the sort that never work and the sort that are always having fights and have relatives coming in from all over the place to make trouble.

Nothing wrong with the blackfellas in our town.

You're lucky. It's a rotten bunch where we are. Not like the full-bloods from up north. They're real Aborigines. Our lot are a bunch of mongrels.

Really? Why is he a bad cop?

Well, he doesn't handle them properly.

Handle them?

Or doesn't handle them at all! Just goes down and talks to them—the blacks—whenever there's a drama, and then goes back to the station and hides.

What kind of drama?

You know, making their noises. Their fuss. Speaking their funny English.

Funny English . . . ?

I should say though that a new constable has arrived in town and he's a big burly bloke and he goes down there and sorts things out!

Sorts things out?

Yes, gives that lazy mob what-for.

What-for . . . ?

A hiding. A good beating! Don't you understand? And the cowards don't dare say anything back, they just slink into their state-housing homes. Which they've wrecked. And as I say, they're lazy. We offered one of them work and he refused! Said the wages weren't good enough. The cheek! We won't make that mistake again.

And he's the good cop? The one who gives hidings?

Yes.

Good-cop bad-cop town?

Yes. But otherwise, it's a lovely town. Strange that you don't know it better. That you don't really know my family.

The door to the surgery opens. The specialist pokes his head in, joking: Gee, I hope you can see better than me! Now . . . Mr. . . . it's time you met with your destiny. Into the chair, please. He's from a different time zone, a different reality. A different religion.

The farmer lifts himself from the bench and turns slightly to the woman, nodding politely. As he follows the specialist through the surgery door he turns and tells the farmer's wife: I once heard a saying, I think it is from a Chinese gentleman, anyway, he said, The further you move away the closer you get. I am not sure what it means, but it seems to fit somehow. Madam, if we were *near* neighbors, we wouldn't know each other. Good luck with your sight.

And with this, the farmer steps deftly back into the light, and the farmer's wife, left alone in the dark, thinks: I should have taken the afternoon appointment instead.

the fable of the gravel pit

★ Toodyay

When his neighbor "let him know," he was furious. He even thought of "outing him," as they say, but that would backfire, for sure. Damaging Samuel that way would only damage himself, though their interaction was thirty years ago. Times were more tolerant, true, but not where the wheat grew short and gnarled, and the sheep collected burrs in their wool, the blight of all shearers in the region. He and Samuel prided themselves on being tough men in a tough place, and it was best left that way. He reflected back to his brief marriage: Samuel had wanted her as well, for keeps, and truth was they'd shared her in the back of Samuel's ute. Everyone knew about that—all their mates drank on it for weeks—but that was okay. Nothing weird about that. He still wasn't sure why he married her—just so Samuel wouldn't, maybe. Anyway, it only lasted a few years, and after the divorce he never heard from her again. He kept the property and she took the money. He had no resentment about that, and nor should he, he thought.

Fair enough. But if she was still around, maybe she would have been a good bargaining chip. Samuel always listened to her. And now it was—in essence—two old bachelor farmers with adjoining properties, helping each other out when need be, but pretty much keeping to themselves, still embarrassed after all these years. Embarrassed that they had so enjoyed each other's company, had wanted to scream and shout about how good it was. But that past was dead and buried.

Samuel had rung and said, I want to let you know before you read it in the paper. I am opening a gravel pit, if I get council approval, and I expect I will, up on the hundred acres next to your two-hundred-acre paddock. You've gotta be joking! he replied. What else could he say? You mean you're gunna dig up that bit of scrub? It's the last bloody bit you've got on your whole damn place. This issue had separated them somewhat as young men—Samuel had cleared and cleared and extracted every bit of lifeblood from his farm, killing the soil with salinity in the end. This was why the gravel was to come. Getting low on funds.

The next call he received from Samuel was somewhat more heated. I can't believe you've done this, Samuel screamed into the phone. You old bastard. To think we were mates once. Okay, bring it on. It's war!

So, Samuel was threatening war. Well, he'd never understand the lengths he was prepared to go to get his own way. He wasn't having any lousy gravel pit next to his farm. And that bit of bush was full of spider orchids and the rare Drummond's gum. He'd always dreamed of making a corridor between the farms so the wildlife could move back and forth with ease—but he had to make do with roos jumping fences because Samuel was having none of that. It wasn't personal, just a different way of doing business, he said. He wondered whatever he had seen in him. Half-thoughts and images came into his mind, of the perfect sculpted body, of his full-forward football body, but he ditched those immediately as ridiculous clichés. Opposites attract, he was smart and sensitive enough to think, but never to say aloud. His wife had said to him once, You enjoyed watching Sam fuck me more than you enjoyed fucking me yourself. He always thought her a coarse woman. There's nothing tough about being coarse, he thought. To her he said, That's not becoming, and she laughed until she was bright red.

So, Samuel was threatening war. He'd predicted that. Second-guessed him. He'd rung around, gone and seen old mates at the pub, even played a game of bowls with a couple of the older councillors. He would call on every ounce of respect he could muster. His family was older than Samuel's; the roots went deep. The very foundations of his house had been laid by the shire president's great-grandfather. Samuel was only second generation, and as such a blow-in. He thought to himself, the best strategy is to strike first and I will. And I have.

It was spring. In a few weeks the fire season would begin and there'd be no mining up there anyway. It would be a hazard in the middle of the drying crops. He watched a flock of Carnaby's cockatoos fly into a stand of wandoo, and grew suddenly afraid. This was unusual. He'd only ever seen them this far northeast once before. They were southern birds that preferred jarrah and marri. They appeared when the rain was coming in, but it was dry and no rain was predicted for days if not weeks. Raucous in the treetops, they suddenly departed and flew north, not south. He rubbed his eyes. It was one of the few times he regretted living alone, regretted not having a really close friend—someone to ring and talk about what it meant. It seemed to him to have religious significance. To be apocalyptic. The next morning, Sunday morning, he went to church as he had done as a child and a teenager. The reading was from Isaiah, but it told him nothing really, though it was about birds and deserts. He knew it was some kind of answer, but he no longer knew how to access it. Even the coincidence was not enough. It left him more bereft.

When he drove up the long gravel driveway to his house, an ominous feeling swept over him and the sky. It was an orange sky. The sun was a sickly red disc in the conflagration. It suddenly crossed his mind that a gravel pit is also known as a borrow pit, and that this was a kind of euphemism. The sky is a sacred text, he said aloud to himself. He drove on past the house to the crest of the hill, and braked. In the distance, up where Samuel's remnant of bush stood, a mushroom-like dust plume rose solid against the orange aura of its declaration. He drove fast towards the fence beside the bush. Samuel was there with a tractor equipped with a ram, crushing and obliterating the bush.

In a fury, he threw open his car door, leapt the barbed-wire fence, and ran in front of the tractor. Samuel looked straight at him, motioned with his face that he was going to continue regardless, then suddenly hit the kill button and cut the motor. They stared at one another through the bloody haze, choking. You mad fuck, Samuel. You can't just go clearing without a permit. Your vengeance is going to cost you heaps, and you won't get the damned gravel pit anyway.

Samuel jumped down from the cab of the tractor and confronted his neighbor, his old friend. You always get your way, you bastard, you always win! he shrieked. They started to wrestle, even throw punches. They writhed on the ground in the damage done. They were scratched and bloodied. Then they were crying and holding each other firmly, holding on for dear life. It's too much, one of them said, it's too much. And the other replied, Loneliness makes bad things happen. We fill the emptiness with nothing. Nothing.

the donation

★ Toodyay

Two years had passed since the fires, and her rebuilt home was finally ready for habitation. It had been a long battle—the insurance company resisted paying the full amount, and the power company had fought hard to avoid paying compensation. Even when it did, it admitted no culpability, though more than suspicion lay on power lines blown in a high wind, in extreme temperatures, coming into contact with scrub. Those had been the worst two years of Isis's life, as they were for friends and acquaintances on the many neighboring blocks and farms who had also suffered the horror of an unstoppable tidal wave of flame.

Isis looked out from her front verandah at the smatterings of green regrowth, the rows of saplings planted by volunteers. Before the fires, it had been a beautiful bush block, replete with marri and wandoo, grasstrees and zamia palms, nestled at the edge of the hills. She had followed all the usual fire precautions, and cleared vegetation from around the house. There was the standard three-meter firebreak around the block. But when the wall of fire came, there was no "defending" the place. She grabbed her kelpie and her laptop and took off in her ute.

As Isis guided the new furniture into place and resisted the urge to feng shui everything, a wave of gratitude swept over her. The community had been very supportive of those who'd lost so much. For two years she'd been living in a donga, provided by a farmer, on the property, drinking from a water tank provided by another farmer (who also carted water for free when it ran dry), making use of a portaloo supplied by a town business, and managing with furniture and household necessities taken from a pool of essentials collected by caring citizens throughout the district. Some of the furniture had become part of her identity, and though she could now replace everything new, she resisted doing so, in homage and affection to those who'd given so readily. From the donga Isis had friends carry out an easy chair, a kitchen table and chairs. The rest she donated to the town's Op Shop.

In the weeks after settling in, Isis made a mission of inviting over many of those who had supported the fire victims, for a cuppa. If there was a little showing off in this, a little affirmation of her new life, it wasn't conscious. It was more likely the recognition that she couldn't have come out the other end without the support of all those around her—those seen and unseen, the overtly active and the anonymous, preferring the shadows as suited their natures. All were wonderful, and all should be acknowledged, and thanked again and again. She was flushed with the joy of acting host in her turn.

So many passed through her new doors, so many hugged her, kissed her, shook her hand and said, *Well done, how courageous, you deserve your second chance.* Isis had tea parties, dinners, even aperitifs. She gave presents to the farmers who provided water and the donga. She offered piano lessons to the children of others she knew had strained their own lives to help her survive.

She needn't have done any of it, and it wasn't expected, she knew that, but it helped her recover, as much as visibly expressing her gratitude. The entire town shared the trauma. Many had been through counseling.

Of course, there are always those one misses when saying thanks, and Isis was very conscious of this. She went to the coordinators of the donation center, set up just after the fire to receive and distribute donations to the needy, the vulnerable. Isis asked, on the quiet, if there was anyone outside the list of names she had, any donors she'd missed. It didn't matter whether she'd personally received their offerings; she was feeling larger than life, appointing herself in the role of making a universal expression of thanks. The coordinators, friends of hers, said, *We shouldn't,* but they did. Another half-dozen names.

Isis sent out invitations saying she'd heard rumors they were donors, and hoped they could pop around for a cuppa and thanks. Four of them politely declined, no doubt peeved their anonymity had been challenged (this was probably paranoia on her part—Isis was certainly a lot more susceptible to this after the fire), but two, who happened to be close friends with each other, responded with enthusiasm. They would be delighted. It was so good to see the district and town back on its feet. They were proud to have helped in their very small ways.

It was a blue, warm morning, but not fire-risk hot, when the donors arrived. Up the long gravel drive, through the charred wandoos with their bizarre green sproutings. Isis would put on a treat, a magnificent morning tea. It was her swan song, though she didn't like that expression. It was to be a rebirth. Start of something new. Isis thought of the phoenix, as she often did, but she dismissed it because there as nothing purifying about the horror fire of two years earlier. Burnt houses didn't make for fertile ash.

The ladies were country ladies, farm ladies in their late fifties, maybe, who quickly pointed out they were members of the Country Women's Association. They were dressed immaculately, as if about to play lawn bowls. Isis could tell her hippie-ish tastes wouldn't be to their liking, but they had manners enough not to comment on the purple drapes, the large mandala painted on the wall, the tiny mirrors in her long, dragging skirts. Kif, her kelpie, ran in and sniffed around their ankles, then took off through a dog flap outside. One of the ladies remarked, We have three kelpies on the farm—all working dogs, we don't let them inside. But even this was said gently, designed for minimum offense and impact.

Isis served the tea on her new china in the kitchen, the gifted table covered with a tablecloth of her own design. The guests admired its intricate patterns. Thank you, she said brightly. It was one I made before the fire—I'd given it to my sister, but when the rebuilding was finished she gave it back and said it was full of positive energy, a way of bridging between my old and new lives. Isis thought she noticed the ladies crook their little fingers more sharply when she said "energy," but she was also aware she might be imagining it.

And so they chatted on, until one of the ladies embarrassed herself, or at least appeared to think so. And her companion shared her shame. It happened so quickly. The lady lifted her arm to illustrate something that deeply interested her, and with a flourish knocked her teacup over. Ever such a small amount sloshed out of the saucer on to the beautiful tablecloth! Don't worry, it will wash out. But the lady was inconsolable and made such a fuss. I will take it and clean it for you, the lady cried. No, no, please just forget about it, said Isis. No, no, let me take a closer look. And with that the lady lifted the cloth to see if it had gone through, and uncovered the table beneath.

There was an eerie silence. The ladies stopped with the cloth poised midair, the offending cup and saucer firmly in hand. They looked at each other stonily. The tablecloth was replaced and patted down, the china replaced. We should go, they said. Oh, Isis said, if it's because of the tablecloth, please don't worry. The lady who had sloshed the tea gave a deep, growling laugh, No, indeed, she said. And with that, they were both out the door and away.

Isis refused to let paranoia rule her life. It was a promise she'd made in this new house, and she meant to keep it. But there was no feeling of resolution after that final expression of thanks. Why the guilt? The tablecloth just didn't matter.

Because Isis had never been able to let things go, she thought maybe she should make each of the ladies a cloth of their own—though she guessed "plain" would be more their style. She was sensitive to such things. Yes, that was the answer. A thanks on top of the thanks. She'd ask her friends from the donation center if they thought this was a good thing to do. Isis wanted reassurance. She'd always wanted reassurance. When the house and the bush had vanished, she was cut adrift in flame and ash. She would never discover what had been burnt out of her, excoriated.

Her friends looked at each other when Isis raised the suggestion.

Why are people doing that round me? Isis asked. What is it that makes people swap meaningful glances I have no damned way of understanding?

The more forthright of her friends decided to end her misery. Direct was best. Sorry, darl, it's just that your gift would be a serious faux pas. A case of a gift horse in the mouth, the other said, not really joking.

They seemed grim, really. Why? Isis asked, bemused.

Because, darl, and there's no easy way of saying this, to quote, they think you are "a greedy grasping hippie—given a new house, new furniture, and you still cling onto the stuff that was donated in goodwill." Including, so it seems, a certain lady's kitchen table, which would "never have been donated if I had known what kind of person would end up with it."

dozer

★ Wundowie

He'd driven dozers for thirty years. From Bobcats to
D10s. As a young bloke, he'd started in a warehouse driving
forklifts. Now, that's an art form. The experienced could whiz
them around on a pin and load a truck faster than an army by
hand. The trick, they said, was in the positioning of the pallets.
He got the hang of it fast, and after a few years was considered
a prize to the company. But then they went bust, and he
branched out. A job came up for a Cat driver—a caterpillar
steel track. He could drive anything, and though he didn't
have *that* ticket, he went anyway. He got the job, and the boss,
being a bit of a crook like so many of them in the "earthworks"
trade, let him drive while he sorted out the credentials. Under
that boss he collected experience and credentials. He became a
gun—a go-anywhere do-anything dozer driver.

Later, he hooked into the mining industry and got to
operate the monster Cat D10 dozer. The bucket was so big
it could have carried most of the things he'd driven before.
Charging a stack of ore—steel jaw and hung guts of the bucket

scraping the ground—he loved the impact with the product. And then the scoop up, the lifting and swallowing. It was brutal, and yet beautiful. Mostly he'd get, You love that power, Matt! We know, we know! But it was never that, it was the getting things done, the efficiency of it. He admired the deftness of the giant, and he felt as if it was an extension of himself. Muscle, sure, but skill in using it. It was the skill, the finesse . . .

He had never been out of work, but industry was under the hammer and he was always conscious that his job might go. The mob he was working for had a bunch of legal cases going on around the world. Like his workmates, he said stuff the greenies, those bastards will protest us out of a job. There'd been toxic spills and damaged environments, but these people seemed not to get it: no mining companies, no modern world to enjoy. But the day did come when the company closed its doors. Not entirely—just their Western Australian operations. Consolidating. We'll be back, they said. Most of his mates spent ages trying to find something else, but he walked into a new job a week later. Ironically, the economy had taken a turn for the better, and a resources and construction boom was just getting started.

His new job was south, way south. He'd been up in the Pilbara—place of Big Machinery—for years. Nice to have a *cool* change! And no more cyclones to worry about.

Ensconced in his cage, he propelled the dozer across the corrugated ground, forcing the great curve of the blade into the ancient jarrah trees. He wasn't used to having so many eyes on him. He didn't care that the greenies hated him, he just wanted to perform well. Whole trees bounced off the cage, though he was deft enough, even in this sluggish brute, to compel the trees to fall into heaps—he rounded them up for the track-loaders to sort out later. Occasionally, one of the longhairs would get in front of the blade and he'd have to stop, but he didn't let it bother him. The cops would drag the longhair off, then he'd start his work again—meticulous, caring.

In thirty years he'd never failed to have a drink after knock-off—at the pub if it was open, or doing night shift, a cold one from the camp fridge, or maybe one from under a roadhouse counter. Near where he was clearing, there was a pub where workers and longhairs drank together. There were regular fights. The longhairs always got the worst of it. He wasn't a fighter, but he'd set in and argue hour on hour, just for the hell of it. The longhairs he argued with were professional "dozer-watchers"—something like trainspotters, they explained. He didn't mind them. He liked trees as well. And he loved birds.

When I was a kid, he explained to one of the longhairs, there was a massive golden oak tree in our suburban backyard. Yes, okay. So I did have a sandpit full of Tonka toys. But do you guys want to hear the story or not? If you do, shut your mouths and listen:

Well, we had this giant golden oak tree out the back. I'd climb it most days, even during bad weather. A variety of birds nested in it, so I'd avoid going up when the eggs had been laid and chicks just hatched. That was seasonal, so it didn't cause me much inconvenience. Then I noticed the same birds coming back to nest year after year, and I got to "know" some of the young'uns. Now, I know I can tell you guys this, because my workmates would be pissing themselves with laughter. But truly, I spoke to them and they spoke with me. My dad said, You spend too much time perched up in that tree like a bloody bird, if you don't chop the wood I'll give you a hiding. I never told him I spoke with the birds, but my mum knew. Once when my dad did give me a hiding for not chopping the wood, I blurted it all out to mum and she rubbed my head and said it's okay, it's okay, I understand. Even now when I visit her—she's old, and in a home—she mentions it.

So why am I a hypocrite? Why do I destroy the birds' habitat? Well, I don't go out destroying just for the hell of it. I do a job that someone else would do worse than me. It'd get done anyway, and a man's got to live. No, no I don't have

a family. Other than my old mum. Never got round to it.
And yes, it could be worse than I do it. As basic as revving
the engines, or walking through the area you're clearing
before work—you know, making a racket, driving things off.
Sometimes I give things a nudge with the dozer, before backing
up and letting it rip.

Inevitably, it'd get raucous, and Matt would tire of the
longhairs' zeal and say his goodnight: see you out there
tomorrow. In a short time he'd almost got addicted to the
drama, the attention. He enjoyed talking—arguing even—with
people outside his profession. He'd always been a workman
with workmates. These longhairs were from another planet.
They were like children—they were himself, or a bit of himself,
not grown up.

The stretch of forest he and his mates were clearing was
to make way for a national highway. He was connecting
east and west. Sometimes he caught sight of a bird or a lizard
going under, but it happened fast and he had to get on with it.
Walking over the area at dusk after knock-off, he stood by the
huge heaps being readied for burning and saw the rainbow of
parrot feathers. Away, at the fenced edge where the longhairs
stood, he could make out a sign saying the last habitat of an
endangered parrot would go under in the next few days. He
shrugged his shoulders.

Work was held up when the dozers and loaders had their
tanks sugared. Some of his workmates planned to go over to
the protest camp in the early morning and give the longhairs
a beating. He said, nah, leave it to the cops. He was pissed off,
though—exquisite pieces of machinery treated like shit. No
respect. Even with the battering they took in the line of duty,
they did the job. He called his machine Enola and loved her.
He'd loved all his machines over the years. They all had names
of the women he'd have liked to meet, or to know more than
briefly. Why Enola? his boss asked. The bomber—she was a
beautiful bird, a piece of art, and yet so brutal, so destructive.

The boss looked at him sideways, thinking him odd but a good worker. He didn't like speaking with the workers more than necessary anyway, and returned to pondering his site map, one foot up on a rock, shorts crisper than an advert.

Enola had been retired. The sugar had killed her off. Matt's new dozer he named Peach. She's a peach, he laughed. The boss said, now, Matt, you go and break that peach in! The boss rubbed his beard and laughed to himself. The machinery was kept in a wired secure area, and Matt nosed Peach out through the gate and towards the forest. Most of the longhairs were gone—arrested, or just given up. A few of the young girls with green hair and tattoos were hanging about, and a couple of camp dogs. One of the blokes he'd told his bird secret to was arguing with the cops: he could see hands waving about all over the place. And then the longhair broke through and was running at Peach, at Matt. The cops were giving chase, but the longhair was like a kangaroo. In a few seconds he'd be in front of the dozer. A slow machine even on flat ground, so Matt had plenty of time to stop. But he didn't. He drove steadily on, straight over the longhair. As shock set instantly in, he heard himself say, I care, I care, I care. No more dozers will create havoc around here. The birds will nest safely, and look after the soul of the longhair.

the graduation

If the Town Hall was not "decked out" for the occasion, it was the next-best. A few balloons floating in the corners, regally attired ushers garnered from the crop of next year's prefects—recently elected to office. The toilets had been spruced up, and an afternoon tea was promised in the foyer for when the event concluded.

It should be made crystal-clear from the beginning that even though his eldest son was graduating, Jeremiah didn't want to go. He had some serious drinking to do, and two hours off the afternoon would stuff the plan. Sure, he could belt it down fast afterwards, but it wasn't the same as that steady drinking towards oblivion that has to start early in the day. But Holly was at him and at him. His eldest daughter. Nineteen, and the apple of his eye. She'd been running the house since her mother's death.

We can't let Samuel go up there to collect his diploma without family to watch him, she pleaded.

Then you go, Holly love, you go and leave me here. I've got things to do.

Dad! Don't even try to pull that one on me.

He knew she'd hide his drink. He was a big man with a violent past, and he'd been known to take it out on Samuel, but he'd never laid a hand on Holly. And he hadn't been rough with his wife. Just the men—there was something he hated about men. His life had been a brawl with other men . . . of all ages, of all sizes, of all origins. His nickname was Ned because of his beard, though Holly called him Jeremiah Johnson, after the wild mountain man she'd seen in an American film. That was her dad—a frontiersman.

Holly managed to keep her dad distracted and sober all morning, and then through lunch, and right up to the time he had to get their old Cadillac out of the shed. The car had been the pride of his life. It was over thirty years old now and run-down. The police in town knew it, of course, and often threatened to yellow or even red-sticker it, but they let it go because Jeremiah, drunken brawler that he was, was never known to drive drunk and never to hit women. These things counted big in a wheatbelt town where there were too many pubs and not enough work. And Jeremiah had been a hard and reliable worker for decades, and if he'd ever seen another man being belted, with the odds stacked against the victim, he'd wade in, overcome his hatred of all men, and lend a hand. The perpetrators, no matter how many, always yelped off, tails between their legs. Then when the victim offered Jeremiah a drink he said, No mate, it's like the song, I drink alone, and then he'd be back to his corner of the bar, to down far too many.

The law of Jeremiah even extended to cops. On more than one occasion over the many years, he had stepped in to look after a cop during a brawl—when it was unfair like that. On the other hand, when the cops had beaten a Nyungar elder, three of them around the poor bloke lying on the street trying to ward off their kicks, Jeremiah stepped in and told them to back off. They did, and rather than his suffering consequences, two of the young blokes involved were mysteriously transferred to a distant town.

That was Jeremiah, but that was back then, before his wife's death. Now he rarely left the couch, and only Holly could get through to him. Samuel—the younger brother she idolized, with his aspirations to go to the city, to a university, and to "make something" of himself—felt angry and alienated and fearful around his father.

The three of them climbed into the old Caddie. The car had been converted to right-hand drive, so though it stuck out as the only car of its type in the region, it also fitted in. Jeremiah had always wanted a left-hand-drive car, but it just didn't work out that way. Samuel, tall and thin at seventeen, sat quietly in the back, just wanting the day to be over. Jeremiah too was in silent mode now. Wouldn't even respond to Holly, who sat upright in the passenger's seat. Crisp today in a spaghetti-strapped red top and black jeans with flat heels, she was a town beauty none of the boys could get near. Of course, they made slurs and suggestions about the nature of her relationship with her disheveled father, but very, very quietly. Rightly, they feared him. He was to be feared. And if it should cross his mind that this was the gossip, the town would never be the same.

People also knew, deep down, that Jeremiah was not capable of what they suggested. It just wasn't in his body chemistry. Nor in Holly's. Girls at school had called Holly the slut only because she was so removed from their world. And she was, as their fathers said repeatedly, "drop-dead gorgeous." But Holly was no one's.

The Town Hall was only ten minutes away, so Jeremiah pulled through the drive-in bottle shop to pick up a flagon of Yalumba. As they drove off, he started unscrewing the top in his lap, and Holly put her hand on his shoulder.

You never have before, Dad, so why start now . . . ?

He handed the flagon to her and she nestled it between her feet.

Samuel cringed and sighed and grew more uncomfortable as they approached the crowd of cars and people outside the

Town Hall. Even the old Caddie embarrassed him. He was cut from different cloth, his mother's cloth. And as much as he loved his sister, she embarrassed him as well. She looked just too "available," no matter what the truth was. He saw men look at her with longing and lust, and he saw the women curl their lips at her. His family was the local freak show.

Why not let Samuel out to find his friends while we find a place to park? said Holly suddenly.

Samuel slunk out of the car and raced across the road, quickly settling in among his friends—the small clique of academic achievers. Many of the boys came from "good" backgrounds. The sons of wealthier farming families, the sons of pharmacists and town councillors.

After they'd parked the car, Holly and Jeremiah found seats at the back of the Town Hall. People turned around and noticed them. Holly smiled pleasantly. Jeremiah folded his hands in front of him and stared straight ahead. The townsfolk gossiped cautiously. Holly overheard one woman say, He has such red eyes and yet hers are sparkling violet. She smiled in the woman's direction, and let it wash over her like nothingness. Jeremiah was so still, you could barely see him breathe.

The graduation ceremony was a slow affair. Everyone stood for the national anthem—even Jeremiah. Holly giggled when the band wandered off-course. She followed the program as the event unfolded, and kept whispering in her father's ear what to expect next. He didn't move at all, and never acknowledged her input, but this didn't faze her at all. She just kept doing what she was doing.

When it came to subject awards, Samuel cleaned up Calculus, Chemistry, Physics, and Biology. Holly was delirious with joy, and *everybody* looked back as she cheered and clapped her brother. Samuel, in agony, felt every cheer and clap. Let this be finished, let this be finished, he muttered. He cast an eye down the back, and even against the lights he could see her animation and, even worse, his father's unmoving hulk of a body. The great red beard, the wrap-around sunnies, the checked flannelette shirt, despite the heat, absurdly pressed like a business shirt by Holly, possessive and obsessive (what *would* become of her . . . ?), the man, even seated, head and shoulders above the audience, like some ancient statue of Baal. At that moment Samuel believed his father was the Devil, that his father was responsible for his mother's death, that there was something unhealthy (too disgusting to think about) going on between Holly and the Devil, the drunken Devil.

Back in his seat among the other students, Samuel dreaded his final call-up. He knew he'd be dux of the school; everyone at school knew. But it was an honor he didn't want—it would take him out on stage for scrutiny one last time in front of the town—Samuel, son of Jeremiah, and brother to Holly.

And the call came. Samuel . . . school dux for 2006! The school roared in approval, the other parents clapped politely, and Holly stood on her seat and yelled, "Right on, bro, right on! Mum would be so proud."

Samuel heard every word. Everyone heard every word. Silence crept across the room. He rushed onto the stage, grabbed his award, paused quickly for the photograph with the principal, and then swished his graduation gown with such a flourish as he turned away that even his closest mates couldn't resist laughing. And the laughter spread. Through the other students, then the teachers, and finally the parents. An uproar of laughter that began benignly, but gradually became mocking and cruel, as if a pent-up sea had broken forth, as if the waves that had parted to let through the chosen son had suddenly closed. He was never one of the chosen, he should never have got so far ahead. Anger drove the laughter to the point of fury. Samuel fainted. The room went silent, except for Holly, who called, Samuel, Samuel . . . ! and sobbed as the teachers tried to lift him to his feet.

He's fine, they said, just a bit overcome by the moment.

All the while, Jeremiah had remained exactly as he was. Unmoved. Waiting for his day to begin elsewhere. Even as they were laughing, he'd remained still. Even as Samuel wilted to the floor, he remained still. But then he heard Holly crying. He'd never heard or seen her like this before. His Rock of Gibraltar, he'd always called her. Nothing bad in that girl at all, he'd once said to his wife. His wife had called Holly an angel.

He turned slowly to study his daughter. She looked ill. It was as if she was melting away. She fell down into her seat, the room watching her as much as the boy on the stage. The freak children. People were saying it out loud now, as if the spell of Jeremiah had been broken. They had nothing to fear from him anymore. The legend was dead. He was just a drunken old pervert who deserved everything he got.

Gently but steadily, Jeremiah put a hand on Holly's slumped shoulder. She settled. He'd never done anything like that before. It was a shock. He leant over and whispered in her ear. They both got up, all eyes on them, and walked up the center aisle to the stage. Jeremiah rocked up the stairs. I'll be taking my son now, he said in a low voice that nonetheless reverberated through the room.

Samuel looked straight at his father, then down at Holly, and then out into the crowd. He seemed suddenly to collect himself, and stepped away from the teachers supporting him. He went straight to the microphone and said, I would like to thank my father and sister for their support over the years, and I would like to dedicate my awards to the memory of my mother.

Then the three of them left the stage, and the aisle seemed broader than ever. No sea could close over it. It was wide open, and the chosen went on their way, out of the hearts and minds of the town. Back at the Caddie, Jeremiah poured the flagon over the gravel and said, I think it's time we moved on, kids . . . Time we saw the world. The kids laughed . . . for they were the children of Jeremiah and knew exactly what he meant.

bad credit

The drive from Y. to N. takes about half an hour. The back road is never busy, so a late-afternoon drive isn't much different from a late-night or early-morning drive. They just ambled their way north, riding sidecar to the almost setting sun.

M. had forgotten her water bottle, so she asked her father if he'd pull over at the deli in town. It is on the main street. Same street as the fitness center. Most businesses are on the main street. He waited in the car as she nipped into the shop. She took longer than he expected, so by way of allaying his anxiety about time he concentrated on a ute ploughing its way over the speed bumps on the other side of the road, heading his way at high speed—or maybe not so high speed, but with the V8 over-revving, it sounded faster.

It was a monster of a vehicle: six spotlights on a roll bar, a steer's head stencil emblazoned across the top of the windscreen, multiple aerials, fat tires, and above the roo bar, set back on the bonnet, displayed in the fashion of prime movers, a blue perspex panel bearing the name of the animal: "BAD CREDIT." The driver was scouring the sidewalks as he progressed—looking for booty. The father prayed his daughter might take that little bit longer in the shop to miss BAD CREDIT's vicious surveillance.

The ute roared past, the guy driving slouched in the pod like an oversized Dalek in his shell—matted hair and aggro attitude, thick arm in checked flannel shirt with torn-off sleeves hanging out the door. The father knew the car's mirrors would be checked, to watch for emergences from the deli, but BAD CREDIT had turned a corner before M. appeared, mineral water in hand.

It'd taken some effort to get M. to take on an evening "steps" class. She was in her final year of school and had a lot of study on her plate. She needs to get some exercise, he said. Sound body and sound mind stuff. This gave M. the shits, and she resisted all the way, but in the end gave in to humor him. And as it turned out, she quite enjoyed it. At first she baulked, because the other "ladies" were a good twenty or thirty years older than her, and would make jokes like, You mean we haven't scared you away yet . . . ?

When she finished a lesson, her body hurt. It was a good kind of hurting, though. The music was a bit dated but okay, and the slightly weird steps teacher was a show in herself. Some of the women dressed up in leotards and the like, but M. just wore her knee-lengths and joggers, and played it all pretty low-key. She was like that—the kids at school thought she was old-fashioned, but she preferred to think of herself as discreet. She wanted to keep her midriff to herself, and didn't much like displaying her bum. This bought her a lot of leeway with her parents, who were proud of her good sense, and generally much relieved of the obvious difficulties of teenage years.

Quietly, though, she quite fancied the boy who worked on the desk at the health studio. He'd graduated from her school a couple of years earlier. At school, he'd never noticed her, though he smiled at her now. She was tall, but he was taller. And that worked for them. He commented on her hair. He talked about music. In the minute or two they had while she signed in and lingered, her father would leave off watching through the glass front of the studio.

The studio was next to the town library, and as it turned out, Monday night was the library's late opening hours. The father would park the car, see his daughter into the studio, then find himself a quiet spot in the library and read detective fiction. He was on a Dashiell Hammett binge and looking forward to picking up where he'd left off.

When his daughter came out of the deli with her bottle of mineral water and got back in the car, he said, We'll get to your steps class just in time, and drove straight down the main street, pushing it slightly harder over the speed bumps as there were no pedestrians around. Dad! I'm going to hit the roof if you go so fast over those bumps. They call them sleeping policemen in England. He laughed—not sleeping now!

He was always making corny jokes like that. She used to say, Shame . . . ! like the other kids at school, but had grown out of it, didn't want to be a sheep. She lived in a district of sheep. Her uncle being a shearer, he'd taught her to take real sheep seriously, Don't call people sheep, they're not . . . people are not as good or intelligent as sheep. She agreed, and through some process of inverted logic came the conclusion that if she didn't behave like a "sheep" at school, she wouldn't insult sheep by usurping their name. M. had never been easy to follow.

Reaching the library carpark, the father indicated to turn, then hit the brakes. What's wrong with you, Dad?! M. said. The father was silent a little too long. Dad? He turned into the car park without saying anything, though she could see he was agitated. He parked, and as if it were some major decision, he pushed his door open and said, Right . . . okay . . . let's go, it's almost started. You know how much you hate being late. M. got out of the car, shaking her head at her father's weirdness.

Her father stood at the window of the studio even longer than usual. Just go, she thought . . . there was almost no time until they started and her talking time was diminishing rapidly. She flashed him a look over her shoulder which meant "you're embarrassing me," and he took the hint, if reluctantly, turning away towards the library while the goofy-looking adolescent serving her dropped his pen.

He stood at the edge of the carpark, taking a deep breath. He walked halfway across, his eyes fixed on the library door. The he stopped, turned sharply, and marched with marked purpose towards BAD CREDIT, parked in a bay on the side where the health studio was. The Dalek had left its shell. The machine gave off an odor of fuel and sweat. It stank. Getting closer, he could smell chemicals—a stench of aftershave or something else that had been sprayed in the cabin. For unlike every other car in town, it was unlocked, with windows down. The confidence of the criminal, he told himself. Without a second thought, he thrust his head inside the monster.

As he'd figured: sheepskin seat covers. Extra gauges on the dashboard. A stereo too powerful for the space. AC/DC and Eagles CDs strewn on the passenger-side floor. Yep, he had this bastard's measure. He half expected to see condom packets strewn around, but maybe they were in the glove box. Suddenly self-conscious, he pulled his head out and stepped back from the ute. He felt sick from the experience. As if he'd warped just a little. He prided himself on being proper in most things, and somehow he'd just crossed the line, joined, if briefly, the enemy.

M.'s class went for an hour. He tried to read, but kept reading the same line over. Normally she'd come in and find him, standing while he finished his paragraph and ensured his bookmark was securely in place. But he couldn't wait that evening. He needed to know where BAD CREDIT was. In the studio, pumping iron. Getting the aggro out. Perving on the girls . . . !

He couldn't cope with it much longer and went out to sit in his car, keeping his eye on the monster. M. was due out in five minutes. It wasn't overly hot—they'd just come out of a heat wave—but he kept changing the car window: down (with his arm out the door), then up with the air-con blasting.

Seven o'clock. She wasn't out.

Then *he* emerged. It had to be him. The hair . . . but then, and the father looked again . . . his joggers had pink stripes on them and he was fluffing himself over with a towel. Not wiping the streams of animal sweat away, but patting himself dry.

A short way behind him, M. appeared, with one of the older "ladies"—they were laughing and carrying on. The father stared. BAD CREDIT had almost reached his machine when he stopped, looked up, and called to the women—called to M. and the older "lady"! See you next week . . . you reckon Annie would let me put *Highway to Hell* on the stereo? We could get some really good moves in with that. The women laughed. The women. There was M., laughing as if she were thirty years old, and there was the older "lady," laughing as if she were thirty years old. And there was BAD CREDIT laughing as well. Not a malicious laugh, just a fun laugh. Kind of like self-irony.

They drove home in the twilight. What's bugging you, Dad? asked M. The father hesitated again—it seemed to be his quirk of the day. Well, nothing really. I was just thinking how proud of you I am. You know, that I am lucky to be your father. That I am glad you're doing this. M. laughed, Yeah, yeah . . . healthy body, healthy mind. They watched a bunch of ring-necked parrots loop alongside the car out of the York gums. Wow, said M., they've really got the moves.

rule in favor

It was great to see his mate after all those years.
They'd "done time" at uni together, worked their way through
law school. We're both from the wrong side of the tracks,
Ron would joke. And he knew he could make the joke. His
wadjela mate was sensitive enough to leave it at that. What
are you doing here? his mate asked. Come to see justice done,
said Ron . . . And you? Got a case this morning. Then they
chatted about their uni days, London, Cambridge, Perth,
mutual friends. They clicked right back into the old patterns
of conversation, but Ron's lawyer mate had to cut it short
saying, You know how it is . . . got to find my client . . . catch
you later . . .

Ron was there for only one case to be heard that morning,
but he sat and listened to the earlier cases out of professional
curiosity. He wasn't sure when his mate was due to appear
as he hadn't thought to ask him about the case in the swirl of
reminiscences. But it was for this case, the third of the morning,
that Ron was in court. He'd been curious how it would go, for

a lot of reasons. His mate appeared and gave him a wry smile. Ron stared back, nonplussed.

The accused looked at Ron, who was one of the few people in the magistrate's court, but didn't recognize him. That well-known hatred of "blacks" didn't even bubble to the surface as the accused remained blank-faced, waiting for the business to be over. Ron laughed to himself, thinking with bitter irony: But then, I am "hard to pick," as he might say. I could pass for white if I wanted to. And I left the town a long time ago, and have rarely been back.

Ron was, however, glad to be back home. He'd wanted to be with family, but work took him overseas for years, and his boyfriend was sick, and Ron hadn't wanted to leave him. His boyfriend had died a year ago in London, and Ron had returned straight home. The accused thinks he "owns" the land that is my people's. He doesn't remember that he chased me time and again from around the edge of "his" lake. But I was a kid then, and to him an Abo was an Abo. Even our wadjela mates who played with us were tarred with the same brush. It makes me sick to put it like that, but all the gloss of racial harmony you hear these days is crap. The town was racist then, and it is now. He watched the accused and waited for the verdict, which he knew before it was made.

Ron'd heard what happened from the kids just the night before. That old white man shot his gun at us, Uncle. We were by the lake. Like Dad says he did when he was a kid—going for a swim in the lake. And when you were a kid, Uncle. We got away like you. He's an old man. There's something wrong with him.

Ron had known the accused for a lifetime. A Big Farmer from an Old Family. One of those families all his people around the area remembered. Ears cut off. Murder. It's handed down, generation on generation.

The accused never went on holidays, rarely left his farm. That was his reputation, and he was proud of it. I was born on my land and I will die on it, he said. He always spat when he said "my land," the accused did. At its center was a freshwater lake—an important freshwater lake. Rare around there. It was going salt, like all the freshwater, but you could still *just* drink it. Fed by creeks and runoff from a big granite rock face. Ancient place.

So the kids went out to the lake when they could—they'd ride their bikes out and hide them in the bush and trek across to the lake for a swim. Sometimes there were speedboats on the lake, and then the kids headed home. The speedboats and their owners and all the others that came with them were from the city. They had an arrangement with the accused. Ron knew about this too.

They are the people I went to university with. They are the people I do business with. Well off. Want their privacy. Don't care about much else. They pay the Big Farmer, the accused. In the city, in legal circles they consider themselves left-of-center. Sympathetic. They even do pro bono work for good causes. They want a solution to the Aboriginal question. They believe in land rights, within reason. I know them.

When they heard that the accused was in a spot of bother with the law, for apparently shooting at Aboriginal kids who had "strayed" onto his land, they called a meeting. If he goes to jail, it will be difficult for us to use the lake. There'll be problems. Best if it's cleared up and forgotten. He says he was just taking potshots at the lake. Didn't see the kids. Wrong place and wrong time—after all, couldn't have expected them to be there. It's private property, and there are "keep out" signs everywhere. Yes, indeed. Indeed. He's been good to us—we owe him.

And Ron listened to the lawyer—his so-called mate— putting the case for the defence. A lawyer who had worked on land rights cases. Black and white together. Textbook appropriate. It made Ron's stomach churn. And the lawyer, though nodding to him with abrupt familiarity, put up a wall straight away and got on with business. And the accused just stared, old and wizened, only looking at Ron when the verdict was due. No jury, just a magistrate and the evidence offered.

Ron wondered later why he didn't stand up against his training and object from the public gallery. This old bastard shot at us as kids. He "winged" my sister. A graze. The police just laughed and told her to stop messing around in the bush, winking at each other.

And that's what it was like when Ron returned home from London. Back to country. With his people. In Cambridge, at King's College, he'd seen the skulls of "Australian Aborigines." At home, the guns were still being fired and the tall tales strung out to be heard through ears cut off by the Big Farmers from Old Families. It was legal then and it was legal now. But "legal" is not law.

That's the story, Ron told himself, leaving the court. His "friend" approached him to take up where their conversation had left off, and was taken aback when Ron lifted his eyebrows and walked off to his car. Words were left hanging in the still, dry air. The gums struggled against the footpaths around the courthouse, sending out their volatile oils. Twenty-eight parrots chattered in the upper branches. At least he knew *they* ruled in *his* favor, and in favor of his nephews and nieces. And that was a fact. That was true. That was the law.

cave visit

It was a long drive but one that had *long* been promised. The children were ecstatic. They asked if their grandmother could come, but Mother said not, because she would find it difficult getting down steps into the cave. She took me there when I was a child, said Mum. Grandma wasn't really *that* old, according to Mum, but she had a bad back at the moment. Another time. We'll go again? the children clamored. Anything is possible.

Glad to be older than her, the boy said to the girl: Grandma escaped the Nazis when she was a little girl, just like you. The girl wasn't sure why he said this so often, as if she hadn't enough brains to remember. I know! she said. But the boy went on: And she lived in a tin shed with lots of others and it was so hot they got sick. But she stayed in the town and she grew up here and then she married Grandpa and her old name was forgotten. She was Polish when she came here, but she's Australian now, he added for good measure. The girl, bored with her brother, continued to play with her paper doll on the lounge-room floor.

Mum called out: Now keep yourselves amused until we're ready. Dad's just putting water in the radiator and checking the oil. The boy leapt on this and bolted out the front door to watch his father get the "old beast" of a car ready for the journey.

Dad had the driver's door open and the radio blaring. He always did that. The boy even recognized the song it was playing, and the program. It was *Macca's Australia All Over*, and the song was by Slim Dusty. His dad had the bonnet perched on his shoulder and was putting the strut in place to hold it. The boy reddened slightly—Dad looked awkward, his one arm, his one hand straining to secure the strut. He looked into his dad's misshapen face and saw what he normally forgot to see, unless kids from school were nearby. A measure of pain hidden under a determination to "make the best—some have it worse." His dad had been "eaten" by a harvester, as he joked. A laborer who'd done what he was told and paid the price. Worker's comp and a disability pension weren't a lot to show for it. Nevertheless, his dad was tall, really tall, the tallest dad in town. Six foot six, Mum would tell him proudly, whenever the boy asked.

Kids in the back, Dad on the passenger's side with his seat pushed right back, making the girl slightly uncomfortable, because the seat pressed against her shoes (Don't kick, girl, don't kick, Dad would say irritably), and Mum driving at that interminably slow pace that sent traffic behind her blasting their horns and giving the finger as they overtook (Dad saying, Ignore them, love, you're doin' just fine). Out through the crops on the verge of harvest, which made everyone sad in different ways. Dad saying, Beautiful crops this year, love to be out there on the header. And Mum adding, wistfully, It smells like bread rising in the oven—the air is full of it this year. And the boy, smart aleck as always: This *car* is like an oven, can we have the air-conditioning on? He meant that sarcastically, for there was no air-conditioning in the old car, other than the windows, which all wound down in response. I like the wind flapping my hair, said the girl, who was pretty but not vain.

They drove the long way, even though the cost of petrol was an issue. But the drive was so interesting, and they didn't often leave Northam. The back way through Toodyay up Julimar Road, down through Chittering, across the Great Northern Highway and down to Yanchep, past the great Pine Plantations, which Dad mumbled about because they drank so much water, and the Gnangara Mound, the great aquifer watering the city of Perth, was getting emptier and emptier. A leisurely Sunday drive after church, Dad said. We've got time. The girl said suddenly, I wish Grandma was with us; I think she looked sad in church. No, no, darling, said Mum, she's just got a sore back so she can't kneel down. You can tell her all about it when you get home. Grandma living two houses away was a real boon for all.

The next tour of Crystal Cave wasn't until two, so they sat on the grass by the lake and ate their sandwiches. The boy threw his crusts at the ducks, and Dad told him off. The boy always begrudged Dad telling him off, but didn't think about why. He threw more crusts, and Dad yelled, Quit it! He stopped then, because other children were looking across at him. Then they looked at Dad eating a sandwich with his one hand, sitting upright like Buddha. Suddenly the boy thought his father intensely ugly.

They were at the cave mouth before the guide, who called everyone as she arrived. Anyone missing? she asked the air. Suddenly a slick new Maserati raced into the carpark and roared its engine before switching off. A man dressed immaculately in designer casuals stepped out, and his two children moved around the seat and out. The girl considered how that man's daughter could have such neat hair when there was no top on the car. Where's the roof? she wondered. The boy's jaw dropped at the car, and he flushed, thinking of their old bomb. The rich family sauntered across and took up their natural position at the front of the group. The guide told them all what to expect below, joking that a tall man like Dad would have to watch out not to bring the ceiling down. Everyone laughed—even Dad. But not the boy.

The cave wasn't deep, about fourteen meters below the surface, but it was the only place in the world where the Crystal Cave crangonyctoid was found. The natural water had dried out, so more was artificially pumped in to keep alive the root mat from the tuart trees on the surface, so the weird microfauna could survive. Mum said, When I came here as a child, there was a lake in here, and water used to drip from the ceiling. Now it was cool and dry and airless.

The guide said water was necessary to make the limestone drip, to form the stalactites and stalagmites. The boy knew this, but he was startled at the idea of microfauna so rare it was nowhere else but where they were standing and walking. Entranced, he momentarily forgot that everyone looked each time Dad bumped his ugly head and said, They didn't design this place for me.

It was going okay until the guide said, Okay, kids, what's that shoal formation look like? Anyone guess? And Dad said, you should know, boy, even *I* can see it.

The boy crumpled to the ground as the rich kids giggled and the rich girl said, It's Bart Simpson and that boy looks like Bart. That was it, he was going. But there was nowhere to go. He shut himself off from the others, retreating into the oxygen-deprived darkness. Where he had walked, now he lurked. The only pleasure he got was when someone said they heard a rat, and a woman screamed and begged to be let out. He enjoyed that.

Then finally they were out again, Dad saying loudly, Well, that was special; bloody sad about the water going. It's those bloody pine trees over the Gnangara Mound—sucking the lifeblood out of everything. Out of the corner of his eye, the boy watched Dad's face melt with each word. He shifted his focus to the Maserati. This was a brand new Maserati Gran Turismo—a convertible with two rear seats. The boy was aware of such things. He had an old matchbox Maserati which he treasured. He was glad Dad didn't know about it.

The rich family brushed past them. The boy found himself side by side with the rich man's son, who turned and said, My father couldn't have bumped his head on anything in there. My mother calls him "the Short Prick." The rich boy's rich dad, hearing his son, put his face down, plunging his hands into his trouser pockets, and stalked to the Maserati, daughter at his heels. Better go, said the rich boy, he'll throw a hissy fit if I "dawdle." He's *such a girl*. And then he was gone, and the Maserati was gone too.

They drove home slowly. Bloody pine trees, said Dad, as they went past the plantations. The girl was humming a tune to herself, looking out of the window, wound up now—it was cooler, a relief. Mum said, You'll have lots to tell Grandma. Then there was silence as they drove and drove until the boy said, If those creatures we couldn't see down there were called microfauna, then Dad must be macrofauna. Everyone laughed, even the girl, just because it felt good, and Dad said, The boy has a real future; he'll be one to watch.

bats

★ York

I don't believe you, she said to him, as the sun sat on the edge of the hill.

It's true, he said emphatically.

And you said this was a mountain and it's really a big hill.

It *is* a mountain, he said. It's over a thousand feet above sea level, and that makes it a mountain.

She stared hard and suspiciously at him, not sure what to say, and finally out of instinct said, I don't think *that* can be right.

What would you know? he said, annoyed. You live in the city right near the beach. You live at sea level. What do *you* know about elevation?

She wasn't entirely sure what he was getting at, but she wasn't going to say so. Instead, she shook her gleaming blonde hair just because it was there to shake, and she thought it'd look special against the sunset.

He noticed. Your hair makes black lines against the sun.

It's not black. There's no black in it. It's a hundred percent blonde. She thought she should be as precise as possible with the boy. What's more, she continued, Mother says it's "translucent." She thought she had him with that word.

That may be true, he said, but with the sun like that your hair blocks the harsh rays and makes it look like a squiggle of black lines.

She was offended now, and no longer wanted to wait for the purple he claimed would fill the sky around the mountain, going into the mountain itself, when the sun dipped below the horizon. She'd asked him why he'd called that *hill* a "purple mountain" and he'd said, I'll show you before dinner. It turns purple most days, especially in summer.

Aware that he'd pushed things too far, he pulled back. He was delighted this girl was visiting from the city, and he tried to regain lost ground by distracting her, rekindling her interest.

At dusk there'll be bats in the sky, he enthused.

Bats? she cried. No!

Yes, bats, he said, pleased with her reaction.

Vampire bats? she asked, incredulous.

He wanted to say yes, to frighten her, but that wouldn't achieve anything. Well, it might in time—over days and weeks—if he had time, but she was there only for the afternoon and evening, so he didn't want to take the risk.

No, no, just plain ol' bats. Dad says they're called Western Free-tailed bats, he said. He respected facts.

They were both silent, and fell to watching the sunset with their own thoughts, their own intensities.

We watch sunsets at the beach all the time, she said. There are so many reds and oranges and purples in so many patterns, especially when it's cloudy. I didn't know the colors reached this far away from the sea.

Yes, it's wonderful, he said, and shortly the mountain will go purple. And then it will be grey and black like the sky. The bats will come in the grey, at dusk. If you throw a rock or a stick high up into the air, they will go for it, thinking it's alive, something they might want to eat. And you can hear them the whole time. You can hear their wings flapping flapping flapping . . .

Soon the two of them would be called into the house
for dinner, and there were mosquitoes about, but they stood
transfixed, caught in the stretching and contracting of time as
the mountain went purple and loomed massive before them,
loomed much greater than any hill could loom, then blackened
as the sky went grey.

I think I can hear a squeaking sound, she said, though she
thought she might be imagining it. She wanted there to be bats.

Bats echolocate, he said seriously, and moved ever so
slightly closer to her. It's how they see in the dark, he confided.
They see with their ears, because they are . . .

Blind as a bat, she said, and they both laughed quietly.

They hear their own sounds come back, he added, after
a moment. They send sounds out of their throats that bounce
off things and come back and tell them the precise shape and
movements. The boy felt his description was getting lost in
the words, so he added, They can *see* an insect flying at night
through their ears.

She believed him. It was truth, she was sure.

Throw a stone up in the air, she said suddenly.

And he did, immediately. In the half-light they saw a small
black entity swoop out of the grey and twist about the stone as
it reached its apogee, before flashing darkly away.

I think there are a lot of bats out this evening, he said
proudly. There'll be heaps later tonight. It's all the Bogong
moths about. They love eating Bogong moths.

This confirmed her growing belief in the boy. On arriving
at the strange house she'd felt revolted to see the verandah
lampshade filled with hundreds of dead moths. It's the Bogong
moths, the boy's mother had said, when the boy was still down
at the machine shed with his father.

Now the girl was really quite happy to be inland. It
was warm and dry-smelling, and the mountain had been
purple. The boy *had* told the truth, and she trusted him in the
thickening dark. He was bigger than her, and seemed someone

she could lean on if she had to, though she'd never have to, she was sure. And there were bats. Best of all, there were bats. She wondered what they looked like, really looked like, up close. And then she shook her hair in the dark-light with excitement, thinking she'd light up the night with her blondeness. She did this for herself, but also for the boy, the mountain and the bats.

And at least one bat heard her. There was a pulling and a tangling and a clawing in her hair, and she screamed a short, stifled scream.

There was a bat tangled in her hair. The boy knew straight away and took her arm and directed her towards the lights of the house. Keep calm, he said, bats often get caught in people's hair. Keep calm or it will tangle worse.

She was sobbing, but his steady matter-of-fact voice kept her calm. She knew the bat must be confused and in terror— this knowledge overrode everything.

The boy was amazed at her "self-control," as his father would have said. *Get some self-control, son!* And here she was, terrified and in pain and in control. It was as if a spell had been cast. She wanted to tell him that she didn't normally swish her hair about, it's just that it was a special day. That it was because of him.

They reached the front door, and he called inside for help. The adults rushed out, her mother instantly upset, her father looking sheepish. Somebody said, Calm, calm . . . scissors, we need scissors. And the scissors were found. Leave plenty of hair around the bat or it will get hurt, the boy said. And the girl, gritting her teeth and fighting the ultimate hair fight, said the same.

Nasty bat, said one of the mothers. And such beautiful hair.

It looks repulsive. Looks like a dead hand. Watch its little claws. And those teeth!

I am sorry, darling, but you're going to be a sight by the time we've got this beastie out, said the boy's mother, all practicality and dexterity.

I don't care! I don't care! exclaimed the girl. I . . . and then she paused to feel the bat clawing and making a distressed sound, maybe echolocating the scissors and her hair and her skin and the blood pumping warm beneath. I want to see it, she said.

Bats are dirty creatures, said the boy's mother. They carry disease. The boy's father squeezed the mother's arm and whispered, You'll frighten her more.

But the girl no longer cared. I want to see it!

And she did—caught in a hank of her hair. Entangled and frightened. She stared at it with wild eyes, then looked to the boy who had been closely watching the operation. Take it, she pleaded with him in a way that made the adults shrink back. Take it and let it go so it can fly back through the dark to reach tomorrow's sunset, to wake when the mountain is purple, to fly into the dusk, the night.

The bat was placed on the verandah, struggling under the moth-light in the net of translucent and blackening hair. It started a slow, agonizing clawing towards the edge of the verandah.

The boy flew from the verandah, through the flywire door, to his room, where he retrieved an old shoebox. By the time he was back, the bat had almost plunged over the edge, watched by the stunned and possessed. Deftly, he scooped it into the box with the lid.

Be careful! his mother said as the boy gently pulled strands of hair away from claws and membranes between limbs, watching the sharp teeth, the tiny half-moon eyes, the veined ears, the fur.

Come inside now, said the girl's mum. You look a fright, darling. She kept saying this as if to soothe herself.

No, please, Mum. I want to see the bat fly free.

So the adults stepped gingerly inside, unsure about everything, watching through the window as the girl and the boy worked together to disentangle the bat.

And then it clawed its way up the wall of the box to the edge as the last strands were extracted, its heart visibly beating in the vein-work, through the fur, mouth open and panting. The boy said, It will remember you forever and it will tell the other bats of the light in the dark, how it really saw you.

She smiled, and reached without thinking to the bald spot on her head.

As the bat suddenly flew into the darkness, they grabbed for each other's hands, and the boy said, I like your hair like that. It looks cool.

in the shade of the shady tree

★ York

The Shady Tree. The Tree at the Center of Town. The Big Fig Tree. The Lovers' Tree. It had a bunch of names, with different age groups favoring different names. It was an old tree, at least sixty years, and long ago seats had been set up under its massive twisting limbs for a quiet and cool moment in this hot, inland wheatbelt town. Even when the fruits came and fell and stained all around, people sat there. At night "the boys" drank and smoked, sometimes "pashed on" with their girls. During the day the town "characters" would sit, watching all that went by, and waiting for acknowledgment and greeting. Ol' Bill had right of way—for a good fifty of the sixty years he'd spent at least an hour on one of the seats every day. The tree was loved and cherished, and was even photographed as part of the authentic heritage look of the town.

Brian "Big Mac" McPherson, however, hated the tree. He owned the land it was on and wanted to build a fast-food joint. It had been his life's vision, ever since his peevish days as a kid when he opined, "Can't get a burger anywhere around here."

He wasn't happy being a country kid, and craved the city. He came from a hardworking family that wasn't flush but made ends meet. They were liked and respected in the district. Brian himself—reliable and polite—didn't seem a bad sort to his elders. But he wasn't liked by his peers. The other kids said he was tight as a tick with his money, was always complaining about them doing things the wrong way, and thought everything about town was "second-rate."

Kerri-ann, the brightest child in school, said, "Brian praises people he wants to get onside, but does the dirty on people he can't get anything from." Kerri-ann was also sharp enough to know that, though Brian gave her a hard time, he was really soft on her. She used that to her advantage if the need arose, but kept him at a distance.

Brian said to her one hot day, sitting under the tree, I'm going to be rich one day and buy this town and make it a suburb of the city—you know, like Distance Education's School of the Air, it will be a school of the city. I want to be able to buy a decent burger. Sheep and cows everywhere, and nothing but pies to be found. Kerri-ann wasn't sure if this was to impress or threaten her, but she felt uncomfortable. After a pause, kicking at the dirt, Brian added, You look like my grandma when she was a girl . . . She let me see her old photo album once. But she keeps it locked away. She says it's her secret life. Kerri-ann wanted to love Brian then, but couldn't. She didn't say anything, and this was pretty well the way it was until he turned up in town again twenty years later, with a fat bank account and a mission.

Kerri-ann had surprised everyone—including herself—by not going on to senior high school and then university. She had left the district high school after year 10 and taken a job in the supermarket. After a few years of listening to You can do better than this, dear, she went for a job at the bank. And there she stayed, looking after the finances of the community. She'd married the manager, had a couple of kids; she belonged to numerous community groups, being the town's chief fundraiser and, in reality, social conscience. The various church groups deferred to her, and though nominally an Anglican, she never hesitated to visit other churches. Astonishingly, she was always made welcome. She had a way of undoing doctrine about her.

As for Brian, his rise had been meteoric. He owned construction and real estate companies. Back when he was at business school, he'd topped his final year. He was one of those guys who bragged that he still had the first cent he'd earned. It was hard to tell whether or not that was the truth. It was possible, and that's what was so unsettling about him. In the business world he was known as a bore—a ruthless but honest and efficient bore. Never satisfied with what he had and never wanting to appear lavish. His single-mindedness drew praise, but his solipsistic and rebarbative nature made him unpopular.

Wives of his business colleagues said he was "sexless," and added, laughing, You'd think he was gay—never looks at a woman . . . but he's not *even* that! He was very tall, very thin, and considered "pinched." There were a lot of verdicts on him, but in their dark and secret places, husbands and wives alike feared his determination, his financial clout, his strange power. They couldn't for the life of them work out what drove him. This was a disturbing mystery.

When Brian turned up in town, Kerri-ann couldn't resist peering through the window of his office on the main street. It was a natural thing to do—she walked past that office a dozen times a day. Why would someone with a chain of real estate agencies set himself up with a single secretary in a small-town branch? Homecoming just didn't add up.

He saw her immediately, as if he had been waiting. Her round face and high cheekbones. Just the same. She sparkled, and it made him feel ill. She'd done something to her hair, beyond ageing or because of it. He had her fixed in his gaze and she had to go in.

Long time . . .

Yep, he said with the same taciturn manner as always.

Missed the place . . . she joked.

No, just some unfinished business. He didn't see any point dragging it out. I am going to develop that open land around the tree.

The Shady Tree?

Yes, then I'm going to install one of my staff in this office and head back to the city. Just wanted to handle this one personally. Make sure it was done properly. I am going to open a fast-food franchise and rather than set the prototype up in the city, I thought I'd start where I started. Where I first lamented the lack of a good burger.

Despite his dead-serious tone, she couldn't believe it. You're joking? No, you're not . . . ? She looked incredulously at him. A recurring disease, like herpes lying dormant for decades and coming back with a vengeance. Why did she think that? She'd never slept around, but she'd heard about it at school. Maybe that was why she'd never slept around. She'd been thinking a lot about the choices she'd made in life. That was to be expected around this age, she consoled herself.

Not sure what to do, she stuttered, W-w-well, we'll see about that! She didn't quite storm off, it wasn't in her, but she was flustered, and marched out into the main street, the sun-hit side, so hot even with the verandah, and almost got herself clipped by a car crossing the road.

In its one hundred and fifty years the town had never seen a protest march. And there was Kerri-ann at the forefront. In the vanguard, she insisted. They started at the tree, marched down the main street four abreast, round the block down to the river, enjoyed the shades and shadows of the little riparian vegetation clinging hard, then back up to the tree. A rectangle. Shopkeepers watched, tourists watched, the town policeman chewed gum, Ol' Bill sat on the seat and saw them off, then welcomed them back again by raising his walking stick.

Really it was a sedate affair—a few banners: Save Our Tree; a few chants: Two Four Six Eight Save Our Tree before IT'S TOO LATE and other mantras that didn't quite add up. Kerri-ann explained about oxymorons, but no one cared. It was the point that mattered.

I know how those longhairs feel now, one elderly protester proffered. Longhairs? thought Kerri-ann. She was becoming more and more convinced she'd made a grave mistake a long time ago. Where am I? she wondered. She concentrated on the cause at hand. Though the marchers probably *did* grow louder and slow down when they went past Brian "Big Mac" McPherson's real estate shop, they were determined not to. Don't make it personal, they'd all agreed. He watched them go past, a smile on his dial, as Kerri-ann's husband pointed out.

Brian "Big Mac" McPherson enjoyed hearing a "doubter" outside his window, after the hoopla had passed, saying, It's none of *my* business . . .

He would act fast. Get the tree down before anyone could do anything serious about it. Something deep inside, he wasn't sure where it came from, niggled at him. The town didn't add up.

His parents had died some years earlier in an accident, his brothers and sisters had moved on. They never felt part of the town, though they'd all been born there. His mum and dad had been born there. His grandmother had outlived her children, and had only passed on ten years back. He missed her, it was true. He'd hoped her treasured old photograph album would find him by right of inheritance, and if not, he ensured it would reach him by managing her deceased estate. She was always proud of his making good, and had him fixed as her executor and main beneficiary when he was still a boy.

Brian will go far, don't you worry, she'd told Kerri-ann one day, without reason. That was in the supermarket when Brian was in senior high school, busing it to a neighboring town. Kerri-ann's grandmother was Brian's grandmother's closest friend. She sensed even then that the two old women had long ago cooked up something involving her and Brian . . .

A town meeting was held, and Brian spoke his piece. The town needed to move ahead with the times, this would bring youth employment, and a tranche of other stock-standard developer arguments. The angry townspeople always brought it back to the mythology, the romanticism, the abstraction, of The Tree. Patiently, he thought, he listened to story after story of love affairs and idle moments, of children playing in its limbs, of people being overseas and recalling their home place by picturing the tree. It made him feel ill. Unless they got government intervention, he knew they didn't have a leg to stand on. He could do what he wanted on that land. The tree wasn't native to the place, it was on private land . . . and, what's more, no matter how much they all went on about it, there was no memory of how and why it was planted. The tree just appeared in memory and was claimed as always having been there. Always there. He was determined, and with the law on his side, called in the necessary workers and machinery. He asked for a police presence.

Strangely, to his mind, on the morning of the clearing, the town was almost deserted. No bodies chained to the tree, no screaming crowds. He noticed the woman who'd said, It's none of my business . . . watching from the corner opposite, transfixed, but that was about it. The local policeman chewed gum, and for a brief moment, Brian felt an anxiety he'd never felt before . . . a form of paranoia. What exactly *was* that cop thinking behind his chewing? Stiffening with resolve, Brian gave the order and the crew went to work. The seats were carefully lifted and transferred to the small town memorial park.

Within a few hours the tree was chopped to the stump and ground to sawdust. The stump itself was excavated in double-quick time. The space was filled in with gravel. Couldn't leave a hole there—it'd be a few months before building work started on the new fast-food store.

Days passed and Brian watched from the window of his office. He even placed his feet on the desk—most uncharacteristic. No one glanced in as they walked past. The town rolled on.

He thought about opening an account in the local bank, Kerri-ann's bank, but decided against it. If she hasn't got enough gumption to come down and shout me out, I'll be damned if I'll go looking for her. He found himself thinking that, and within twenty-four hours had installed his replacement and headed back to his city offices in one of the tall buildings on the Terrace.

Some time later, Brian's assistant handed him a large package. I didn't open this one, sir, as it's marked "private."

Brian looked at it quizzically, leant over his desk, and sliced it open with a paper knife. It was his grandmother's photograph album, and a letter had been inserted between the front cover and first page in such a way that it peered out and couldn't be missed. He felt a warmth as he touched the album, such as he hadn't felt since being a child. It was affirming. He smiled with his entire body. It was as if all the waiting, all the preparation, had been resolved. The letter. He was curious. He would thank the sender. He was certain of that . . .

Dear Brian

> *You should have this. My grandmother recently passed away and I ended up with a number of her personal effects, including this photograph album. Grandma said in her will that she had been given it by your grandmother during her final sickness. They were close, as you know. I was browsing through the album—it is full of photos of you and me playing as children . . . I'd forgotten how much time we spent together before starting school—and I came across a photo that meant a lot to me, and might mean something to you. It's on the second page, bottom right corner.*

> *Sincerely,*
> *Kerri-ann*

He smarted. That's how I sign letters, not how she should sign letters. It also annoyed him that there was no attack, no detectable sarcasm. What about the triumph of burgery over the town? What about his nickname, Brian "Big Mac" McPherson, inculcated through hate mail?

He looked out of the plate-glass windows onto the river far below. Yachts. The smoky glass made it all seem cool and relaxed. His colleagues' Wednesday afternoon sailing. Later, they'd be drinking it up at the club. He'd poke his head in, drink a shandy, talk business when their guard was down, and leave.

He opened the first page of the album. His grandmother as a young woman. His grandfather. Before they were married. They were a handsome couple. Slowly he turned the page, as if in no hurry to reach anything. He half looked at the bottom right corner, then looked again, longer, with more concentration. He glanced down at the yachts again and realized nothing was moving. It was suddenly a flat, dull, windless day on the river. He looked back at the photo and drummed on his forehead with his fingers. His grandmother and grandfather planting a tree. Where had they got it from? Not a tiny sapling, but a small tree—already twisted and writhing and reaching out with its shade. He could see the birth of the shade of the shady tree. A flesh-and-blood tree, held by both of them: their arteries, their skin, their hair growing together. Those jokers with their toys. Sailing pointlessly about, dragging shadows around with them. Well, that's what it comes down to: something has knocked the wind right out of their sails, and they're going nowhere fast.

drive

★ York

He checked the saplings out front and then went back inside. Eucalypts, they'd made it through the summer and were looking sturdy. It was his achievement, his reason for being outside, with the paddocks spreading around. The place was an island, and the trees would grow to screen out the unwanted. He looked through the window at them, vigorous alongside the gravel drive. Yes, they would survive. He flicked on the television—news, a game show. He switched it off again and heard the cross-cutting peals of pink and greys lifting suddenly as a flock: they aren't just raucous, he thought, they are modern. They work together by working against each other. They are making new mythologies, as well as the old. Timeless. Silence.

Then a rumbling, a sound he hasn't heard for years. He looks outside and jolts. He is suddenly out the door screaming, Fuck me dead! as a dozen horses gallop towards the saplings, halting just before them, and he sees the eucalyptus leaves tremble. The horses—mares and geldings—start tearing chunks of dried wild oats and radishes out of the dirt. Slowly they calm

148

down, they concentrate on their eating. He sees the shire ranger is on the drive, and behind her the "horse woman," his neighbor. They are working around the horses to drive them back up onto the road.

In a decade he's only talked with the Horse Woman on four or five occasions. She's always out in the paddocks or on the road, riding, with her strapper following: a girl of a certain age, always the same age, year in year out, thin and sullen, who can tame the wildest horse. He sees the Horse Woman most days, of course—in the distance, riding past . . . calling to her horses, yelling at the strapper . . . but they've only spoken those few times. They don't even greet each other as he drives slowly past her riding along the gravel shoulders.

The Horse Woman starts to yell at her horses. Down the road there are cop cars blocking "exit holes": the T junction, gateways. This is obviously a *major incident.* It all slows down for him, and he looks past the ranger, who is moving cautiously, at his neighbor: she is tough and small. In her riding pants she looks asexual. He has never thought of her as being separate from her horses. Their immensity against her slightness. She has a reputation around town, and no one bothers her. She has trained stayers and bolters. By her house, she keeps the great stallions that service the mares. In the paddocks behind his house most years there are foals gambolling. He finds this soothing.

The Horse Woman gets behind the horses, and he walks closer. The ranger calls to him to block the top of the drive— We'll drive them out the other side where the fence is down. He asks what has happened. Someone left a gate open . . . He senses the ranger's disgust. We found them halfway to town. Not the first time.

Years ago, the last time he spoke to the Horse Woman, it was after someone had shot one of the horses. Horses bring out the best and worst in people, he thought. Horses aggravate humans like no other animals, strangely . . . he wondered why. He had been around horses, vaguely, indirectly, his whole life, and could head them off without a problem. He watched the Horse Woman get behind them. Get on! Get on! Whoowhoo whoo! Whoowhoowhoo! Ya! Ya! she called. Then she whistled like he'd whistled with his brother when they were young, driving the sheep towards the shed. Horses respond like sheep, he thought. They leapt and kicked, then ignored the calls and started eating again. One broke away towards him, and he could see it was the leader so the others would follow. So quiet now, so unused to speaking to people . . . he found it in himself to call at the horses. Get back! Get back! Ya ya ya! He clapped his hands. He'd always been embarrassed doing this, but he felt good about it now. He yelled louder and louder, so much so the ranger stopped her driving and looked at him. He didn't let it stop him.

The Horse Woman was right behind them now, and he could see the sinews of her neck working hard as she yelled. He noticed she had blonde highlights through her hair. Never thought how old she is. . . . maybe fifty, but it's hard to tell . . . skin exposed to the season, like her horses. Maybe she was younger, or older. The horses stopped dead still, eating, swishing their tails. Then, abruptly, she picked up a paddy melon and threw it at an old mare. The melon—noxious infesting weed in those parts, that he thought he'd removed entirely from the block—burst over the flank of the old mare, which kicked and bolted, Ya, get a move on, you old bitch, you old slut . . . called the Horse Woman, liquid and pale unformed seeds spilling down the mare's flank, leg. Since she was not the lead horse, the group compacted with the mare's charge and stood their ground. The Horse Woman picked up another missed melon, and he opened his mouth to say, No!, but nothing came out. He felt like that statue, *The Caller* . . . the mouth shaped, the intention written in the features, but eternal silence. He saw the ranger semi-laughing. The next salvo hit the lead gelding: Move, ya fuckin old whore . . . bitch slut . . . move ya ball-less wonder! With that, the horses charged onto the road and down the bitumen towards the police cars blocking the town end of the T junction.

Mesmerized, he was drawn along behind them and caught up to the Horse Woman. Do you still want help? he muttered. Yes, block any holes you see. She didn't look at him. Driving them back towards their paddock under the hill, he worked alongside her, calling and clapping. He noticed that some of the older horses had numbers written on their shoulders: not branded, but something close to that. He feared for them, the old bitches.

He was hot, his heart pumping, and kept calling even as the horses trotted in a mannered way towards their place. Behind him, cop cars that had come from around the district, called in by the ranger as part of a general SOS, rolled slowly as backup, calling out to the ranger, telling her it was good exercise and that they'd signed up with the force just to witness such occasions. The horses slipped through the gate in single file, and then fanned out at a gallop, all of them suddenly lead horses, looking relieved to be there. The strapper—different face, but same age—was at the gate and closed it behind them. He spoke to the sullen girl, her eyes downcast, conscious the Horse Woman was looking closely. He remembered the story of how the Horse Woman was said to watch her animals mate, and felt uncomfortable. He said quickly to the girl, you better lock it up tight. The girl said something indecipherable back and didn't look at him.

He retreated and stood near the Horse Woman. She turned to one of the cops, who had just emerged from a patrol car. Locked it after I was in there this morning. It's been opened. I've lost three gallopers over the years—shot. Found bullet shells up here the other day. He spoke then: I heard a shot a few weeks ago. I rang the police. They said not to worry, it's the country, what do you expect. But I've been here all my life, and I know there are places you don't hear shots. Yes, I heard that—it was a high-caliber rifle, the woman said . . . thanks for ringing the cops, maybe they'll work out that there's a pattern to this. Don't ask us, said a police sergeant, we're from out of town! The Horse

Woman ignored him and spoke to her neighbor again. Spoke to *him*. Remember, years ago, after one of my horses was shot, you said you heard shots then as well. I did, he said, the horses are in the paddock behind me, my house is closest to them. I listen out for them.

The cops melted away, and the ranger went off to file a report, and the strapper walked into the paddock, wandering nowhere in particular. The Horse Woman looked at her reclusive neighbor—he was dripping sweat and panting. Want a lift back up to your place? she asked. He hesitated, slightly—*she* didn't have a drop of sweat on her, and her breath was the same as always. Took it out of me! he laughed. Jump in then, she said, brushing past him as she opened the passenger door. He felt a different heat rise in him—he stepped back: No, no . . . I'll be right . . . still a bit of gallop left in these legs. He felt her staring at him as he headed back up to his place. Those horses are a lot of work for her, he thought. But then the saplings, their resilience. Winter was almost there, and steady rains were predicted.

eyewitness

The sublime artist must flee from details.

—Stendhal, *History of Painting*

★ York

They came in the early hours of the morning to bring down the tree. To cover the sound of the chainsaw, the father had his boys rev the shit out of their motorbikes. He was a man who loathed hoons, but when needs must . . .

The tree was a cause célèbre in town. It was as old as the town's oldest citizen, and though it wasn't native, it felt as if it belonged. That's what everyone said. And to support the case for "saving the tree," the most vocal supporters pointed to the fact that one of the most respected Nyungar elders also defended the tree. Not that the tree's enemies thought this carried much weight. Never does when it comes to "official" land ownership arguments around here. The owners just wanted the tree gone because it was right where they wanted to build a fast-food shop. A fast-food shop in a "picturesque" country town. A huge shady tree with seats beneath where old and young sheltered from extreme summer heat. In one way or another, all the town's buttons had been pushed over the question. The issue went all the way to the state parliament. It made the big state newspaper. It dragged on and on, said the owners, who were bitter, and fumed that landowning meant nothing.

These were the "facts," as everyone round about knew. So when Baz woke up behind the pub, where he had crashed out after staggering through the back door at closing time, and started slowly to drag himself home, he knew what was up, no matter how dazed he felt. He stood there and watched it happen. The tree "removalists" saw him standing and watching, but they kept on at it. The headlights of utes and motorbikes shone on the tree, and the noise was incredible. Huge limb by huge limb, the old ficus tree fell. They went for about an hour, slicing it up like an onion. That was the best description Baz could muster at the time. Like an onion.

Since there had been a preservation order on the tree, the police became involved. They cautiously asked around, though I guess they knew, as well as anyone, what had happened. It was an open secret, but there were "no witnesses." Everyone would say, Well, we heard *something,* but it just sounded like the local hoons at it again. We are used to it. The police usually break it up on the weekend. This was a Monday night, though, and out in the country it's not as simple as calling the cops, who were probably in bed, vaguely hearing the racket in the distance and wishing it would go away. I mean, that must be it, because it's actually what happened. No one owned up, of course, and no one reported seeing anything at all.

At first, Baz laughed about it, and said nothing. He was feeling pretty crook when he woke, and after that, it was a rough day at work. At the pub that night, he listened to the gossip and made no comment, but when anyone mentioned the removal of the tree, he laughed in the kind of way that made them look twice.

Still, things got pretty heated around town, and arguments and even fights broke out over what had happened. The family whose land it was, who'd been trying so hard to get permission to remove the tree, had gone on holiday. All of them. They were a farming family, and the boys worked on the farm as well as the dad, and as it was almost the start of harvest, it was an odd time to be away. Something about the cloak-and-dagger nature of it all got to Baz. He felt annoyed at first, then angry. He wasn't even really sure why. He couldn't give a damn about any old tree. He'd never sat under it, that was for sure. But then he thought back to his childhood, and recalled how often he had played around that tree. It was a giant even then. A door had opened to his past. It came back in a flood and it made him angry in so many different ways. He didn't want to think about it!

A week later, Baz walked into the cop shop and told them he wanted to make a statement. The police knew Baz well—he was a good sort really, they'd say, though he was a drunk and often boisterous around closing time. But small towns and all that! You put up with it. Necessary, really. Part of the fabric . . .

When it came to filling out the witness statement, Baz was stumped. I can't just write: it looked like an onion being sliced up. I need to be precise. What was really strange was, though he knew the father and sons well, he didn't want to name them—he'd just describe them. Wasn't going to use any names. That seemed too close to plain old dobbing to him. He tried to see them in his mind's eye, but they wouldn't appear.

He'd never taken much notice of the way people looked. I mean, yeah, he could say if they were a man or a woman, maybe if they were black or white, but even that didn't concern him much, which is more than you can say about most people in the town. Shades of skin color are a big issue around there. Okay, they were blokes, and the guy with the chainsaw was an older bloke, and the boys on the motorbikes were younger. Hold on, wearing helmets . . . couldn't really tell how old. They *seemed* younger. There was another boy helping out with the sawing—pulling with ropes at limbs being severed. He looked about twenty. Long hair. Tall. Medium build. That was it. Baz was feeling inspired now. Four of them. What were they wearing . . . ? Well, they were blokes wearing what blokes wear on such an evening. Not hot, but not cold either. Boots, jeans, maybe checked work shirts . . . There was a lot of glare from the headlights. There were two utes—Toyota pickups, ninety-ish models . . . and two trail bikes. About 500 cc. A chainsaw. Not sure what sort. The fella cuttin' had earmuffs on. Faces of the two I could sort of see? I know those faces so well. What *do* they look like? Eyes? Well, we used to call the old man "Baby Blue Eyes" at school to rile him up. I guess he's got blue eyes. I'll put down "the fella with the chainsaw had blue eyes."

And that was it. He didn't have any more to add. He signed the document, handed it to the police, and headed off to the pub.

Nothing came of any of it, really. No one was prosecuted. The defenders of the tree licked their wounds, but got some satisfaction when planning approval for the fast-food shop was turned down. The argument was, it would damage the heritage profile of the town, which was true, but also, built into the decision, there was some appeasement of the many citizens disgruntled over what had happened. Surely. People told themselves this anyway. The feeling of powerlessness is difficult to cope with.

But there was a minor subplot to the narrative—nothing ever completely resolved itself in this town. The old man and his boys who'd killed the tree confronted Baz some time after their building plans were turned down. They bailed him up in the main street, in the early hours, when Baz had woken up from his usual stupor out the back of the pub and was making his way home. They had been drinking at home and had decided to go out and find him, tempers accruing over the evening. They knew his patterns. Everyone knew Baz's patterns.

The car pulled over and the four got out and confronted Baz. A single streetlamp cast a low light on the corner. Baz asked them what they wanted. You dobbed us in, you drunken old bastard, one of the boys said. Yeah, yeah! they said together. Baz grabbed for the lamppost, but missed and fell over. That broke the ice. The other blokes laughed. Ah, he's not worth it, the old bloke said. Baz stared up at the men. What are you lookin' at, old man? said one of the boys, pushing Baz down with a boot to his chest. Baz lifted his head again. Well, he mumbled, I was just lookin' at your eyes. Hard to see in this light. Seems to me you're a family of babies . . . The boy put his full weight on to his boot and Baz fell back and cracked his head. Come on, said the old man, let's go. Baz propped himself up on an elbow as the family walked away. He called into the dark that was swallowing them, Just a family of baby blue eyes, that's all . . . baby blue eyes! And that was as far as it could go.

the purple suit

It was two years since Solomon's father's "accident." Two years to the day when the invitation to the harvest ball arrived. The ball was to be a formal affair—one sponsored by the Shire from its mysterious "entertainment" fund, various town businesses, and a few of the richer farmers who'd had bumper seasons. For once, it had been a year of perfect weather. Rain had fallen—plenty but not too much—storms had stayed away, and wheat prices were high. Not like the year Solomon's father had died—it was bones-of-your-bum drought that year, and foreclosures were routine.

The small house Solomon now lived in with his mum was a far cry from the great rambling farmhouse out on Broad Dales they'd once occupied as a family. But he tried not to think about that, tried not to compare. It was the easiest thing to do. There was before, and there was after. And this was after.

He didn't want to go to the ball, but he felt he owed his mum. She wouldn't go with another man—he knew that and it pleased him—but he knew the price of loyalty to his dead father, and his loyalty to her as the "male in her life," was accompanying her to the ball. That was socially acceptable, socially appropriate. Solomon was a very proper fourteen-year-old who didn't see himself as like his peers in any way. He didn't drink, smoke, or "finger" girls on the school bus. He planned to go to university, study law, and eventually buy back Broad Dales, whose loss, along with his father's death, was sediment at the bottom of his life.

There was no money to buy a suit for Solomon, but all agreed he must have one. His mother wouldn't have minded if he'd gone in his jeans and a crisp shirt, but there was to be none of that. His mum's clothes were dated but good quality. His parents had been icons of the town, the perfect couple, and the town wheeled them out on special occasions for admiration. Stalwart, reliable, and handsome.

Solomon spent the morning walking along the river. It was just starting to turn with the heat, to settle to a mixture of dry stretches where it had been "trained" to prevent flooding, and the few remaining "permanent" waterholes. The waterholes were linked with algae-thick, stagnant streams, though by the town itself there was a long, deep stretch of water that kids still swam in, despite signs warning of amoebic meningitis in fading red letters, dented and bent with assault by stones. He carried a sketchbook with him and added to his paper aviary of birds. That morning he saw two spoonbills, an egret with feathers whiter than how he imagined snow, a white-faced heron, and a group of small waders he couldn't quite identify at a distance, but guessed would be plovers come out of the stubble to the edge of the river. There were many other birds he didn't sketch.

Walking in again through the back door, he saw it straight away, stretched out on tissue paper on the Formica kitchen table. The purple suit.

What do you think? asked his mum.

He said nothing, but walked across to the piano, crammed into the kitchen with most things they owned, and dropped his sketchbook on top of the instrument with the piles of sheet music. He noticed a grade one book and guessed that Mrs. Crest's daughter had been in for a lesson. The town's worthy sent their young ones to his mother for lessons, to help out. It pained him. *Rum tum, tum, rum tum, tum, listen to the big bass drum . . .* over and over.

It's not just a loan, Solomon, it's a gift from Mrs. Crest. It was her eldest, Dean's old suit. He doesn't wear it any more. It's in perfect condition; he just grew out of it.

Solomon's nemesis, Dean. Dean was always kind, but made him feel it. Four years older, Dean was now in the city at the Mining School. He was ambitious and going to be rich. His whole family was ambitious. They were "townies," not farmers. Mr. Crest, bank manager, sat on the boards of the local supermarket, the district newspaper, and no doubt the harvest ball committee. Solomon cringed. But seeing his mother droop, he said, Thanks, Mum. I will write a note to Mrs. Crest.

The dutiful son took the purple suit, carefully, on its bed of tissue paper, to his room, where he placed it on hangers and suspended it across the narrow oval mirror of his chipboard-and-masonite wardrobe. He knew his every movement, his every echolocation of what he lacked—what *they* lacked—exaggerated the pathos. He was proud in the bubble of his own pity. Purple rayon suit on old chipboard and masonite, he told himself. He scrunched up the tissue paper and hurled it into his wastepaper bin. Flopping on the bed, he hooked an arm beneath the candlewick cover fringing the floor and grabbed a book from underneath without looking. Here during school term he did his homework, or when Mum wasn't teaching piano, at the kitchen table.

Rather than falling sick on the day of the ball, Solomon started getting sick a few days before, and easing into it. That would prepare his mother for the disappointment. Stomach cramps, dizziness, gagging, but not too much—not enough to go to the doctor, though his mother kept insisting. No, no, it will pass. It got slightly worse each day.

But worse, what made him genuinely ill was that his mother just came out with it and said, I know you're ashamed to wear that suit, I know that Mrs. Crest's son will be at the ball and will feel superior to you, I know what the Crests are like, and I know that suit is out of fashion. You will stick out like a sore thumb. Everyone will notice you, and I know how much you hate being noticed.

That was brutal. His mum could be like that. She wasn't all sweetness and light. She wasn't a downtrodden widow who absorbed everyone's pity to make her life liveable. She knew the truth of the town, she knew the truth of the families who sent their little talentless ones to plunk the keys for the first three grades before they found a more professional teacher to further dreams of cultural capital. She knew those who helped "take the farm off her hands" didn't give a shit about her or her son. She knew her husband's death was an accident: his tractor had overturned, one of those accidents that in any other industry would have come under scrutiny. Only the country doesn't protect its own.

And anyway, his mother continued—Solomon still dumbfounded, a dying duck on his candlewick—Anyway, I think I'll go on my own. I'd prefer it. I might cut my wedding dress up, turn it into a Vivienne Westwood mini. With no underwear.

Solomon blushed. He squirmed.

Sorry, darling, didn't mean to make you feel uncomfortable. Just thinking aloud.

Solomon thought his mum had cracked, had finally lost the plot. The strain had got to her.

I'm feeling better, he said, I'll be right. It rushed out of him.

You'll look fine in that suit, his mother said without appeasement, without thanks. Walking back into the kitchen through his bedroom door, she added, You'll look more than fine, Solomon, you'll look like your father. He was always the one who stood out.

They walked the couple of kilometers to the ball, having refused a lift from Mrs. Crest, who poked her head through the back door in her finery to offer it. Seeing Solomon first in the purple suit, she said, My, I think you shine brighter than our Dean ever shone in that outfit. She inflected "outfit" in a clownish fashion. He'll be there tonight, she added, he will be delighted to see his old suit put to such good use!

When Solomon's mother appeared, Mrs. Crest looked genuinely shocked, Well, you've turned the clock back, my dear! You were always the belle of the ball. Solomon noted that there was no sarcasm in Mrs. Crest's voice, and if there was, it had caught in the throat and was stuck there. Mrs. Crest's gown, stylish and costly, was recently purchased, whereas his mother was wearing a silver lamé gown of twenty years ago. It wasn't a Vivienne Westwood shocker, but it was a surprise, and *would* stick out like a sore thumb. A sore thumb that made people jealous.

Solomon had never drunk alcohol before, but that night he downed sherry after sherry. He watched his mother dance with men he knew she despised, and absorbed polite barbs from Dean and impolite barbs from his schoolmates. He'd cop it first day back at school. They all caught the bus to travel the sixty kilometers to the senior high school, so he wouldn't be able to get away with it before or after school. Fashionable, one girl said. Sharp, one of the overdeveloped rich cockies' sons said. Solomon was no longer counted as a farmer's son. A dead farmer is okay, but no land meant no status in that world. He drank and looked supercilious. He didn't get out of control; he didn't vomit. He just stood watching his mother go round and round making a fool of herself. Not that she did anything "odd" or "wrong." Rather, she enjoyed herself.

They walked home after the ball. Solomon felt a little heavy, but didn't think the alcohol had had much effect on him.

You shouldn't drink, Solomon, it makes you more sad and dour than you are.

The fresh air started to go to his head. I think you imagined you were wearing that Vivienne Westwood dress you mentioned, Mum. Having fantasies about all those men mauling you.

His face stung. His mother had slapped him. She had never hit him in her life. His father had belted him. He burst into tears.

Why did Dad hit me so much? he yelled at her. Why didn't you stop him?

Blood trickled from his lip. He tasted it through the sherry, could feel its warmth. It dripped down onto the purple suit and was lost in the dye and moonlight. The night was bright. If anything, it simply cast a shadow over the jacket.

His mother didn't apologize. She didn't say anything for a while. And when she did, it was simply, Come on, keep up, it's time we got home to bed. I've got lessons to give in the morning. And that suit will need to be dry-cleaned. I think it's done its duty. We might give it back to Mrs. Crest, even if she doesn't want it.

Moonlight singed the hair on the back of Solomon's neck. His jacket collar rubbed. He identified the mo-poke call of a bird—a tawny frogmouth— in the great York gum they walked under. And then he cried a little as his mother said, Mr. Crest is a good dancer . . . it must pain him that Mrs. Crest dances so poorly.

parade

The big people were fussing about, lining them all up. They looked across at each other and gripped their trike handles hard. Festooned with Christmas decorations, the trikes were mighty machines. Both of them wanted to speak, but the overwhelming presence of their mothers kept them from doing so. Nervous and excited, they wanted to set off into the hot street, but were held back by gentle hands on their shoulders.

Then she said to him, I like the streamers coming out of your bike.

And he, embarrassed without quite knowing why, replied, My Nan put them there. His mother leaned down and whispered something in his ear, and he added, And you've got good streamers too.

They knew each other from kindy, but not well. The boy knew she was three months younger than him because he knew everybody in the world's birthdays.

They looked at each other out of the corner of their eyes. Mainly studying the trikes, and noting the inadequacies of their own, or being proud of the bits that were better. Both were listening out, vaguely, to their mothers chatting.

It's a stinker of a day, one mum said. The other agreed. And they sounded as if they were telling someone off when they said, It's always so hot at this time of year, they should hold the parade in the cool of the evening. Not in the middle of the day. It must be a hundred and three on the old scale out there now. Yes, not good for the children and the old people. And then they went quiet and chewed their lips and nails, glancing down at the children.

I've got a new hat, the girl said.

I've got lots of sun cream on so I won't burn.

So have I, said the girl. You need a new hat.

It still works, this one, the one on my noggin, the boy said to his foot toying with the pedal, eager to get going.

And then they were going, out from under the shade of the great gums. The entire parade was tumbling down to the corner outside the town hall, getting ready to turn onto the main street, to greet and reward the public. The parade's organizers called out the names of individuals and groups when it was their turn to join the tail of the procession. The local fire-brigade chief was at the head of them all, twirling a baton.

But the two children on their trikes, and their mothers standing vigilant behind them, got pushed aside in the enthusiasm and confusion as the band marched past, and the local ballet group did pirouettes, chassés, and jetés towards their audience. Following at a snail's pace was a painfully red historic fire engine, upon which was mounted a puffing and sweating Santa, weighed down in a costume ten times thicker than anyone's else's, like some fantasy of ice in the mirages that warped the road, clutching a sack of sweets to hurl onto the pavement for the town's kids to squabble over and collect.

It was *so* hot. Those ballerinas should slow down, said someone, they'll collapse before they even reach the corner. It's the hottest parade day ever!

Then various farm animals were dragged into the procession, panting and lolling their heads as if about to expire. It's cruel, someone else said.

The entire procession was moving, the lead contingent around the corner and well on its way down the main street. The trike-riding children could hear the clapping and cheering and laughter. But each second it got softer, and by the time their mothers managed to attach them to the very end of the parade, like pinning the tail on the donkey, the applause had given way to the noise of the parade itself.

It's so hot, said one mum, the kids really shouldn't be riding.

That's true, said the other. Come on kids, let's give it a miss and do it next year instead, it's too hot this year.

No, muuuummm! I want to. We want to! The boy and the girl looked at each other, speaking their secret language of kinship, and started pedaling furiously.

Slow down, slow down. Okay. You can do it, but ride slowly so you don't make yourself sick.

The children were no longer feeling the heat, though they sweated and panted like Santa and the farm animals.

The boy had thought he should lead the girl. He didn't know why, but thought it best because the other kindy boys would see him. Maybe that was the reason, the other boys. It didn't seem a real reason to him, but an idea that should be obeyed. But the girl had pedaled out ahead of him, in her own world of streamers and whirligig reflectors flashing on the trike's wheels, on the pedals, and in the heels of her sneakers. The other girls would see her and admire her "fashion." She knew about fashion. But then she looked over her shoulder at the boy, and that slowed her down, and he went past. Well, she wasn't going to race him. She didn't care!

The procession was slowing down, the parade was wilting by the time the boy and the girl cycled onto the main street. They were feeling sticky and tired, and after waves from a few old folk from the hospital, sitting under the shade of shop awnings, they felt they had done enough. Gradually their trikes wandered off at an angle and they jammed wheels against curb. Their mothers directed them back to the line.

Frayed by the heat, people started to laugh at the children. Slow, sarcastic laughter. Some took photos, but not because they found them cute. The mothers looked daggers at their friends, their fellow citizens.

All the lollies will have gone from Santa's bag, said the girl.

They'll all be melted and horrible anyway, said the boy.

Yes, said the girl, now scooting along with her feet rather than using the pedals.

They stopped, but they had reached the end of the street anyway. The procession had broken up, and the parade was finishing. There would be speeches now. The children were to go to the park for games, and to meet Santa.

I don't want to go to the park, the boy said to his mum. It's too hot.

I think we'll head home to the cool now, one mum said to the other.

Yes, us too. That's enough for today.

The boy pulled the streamers from one side of his bike and handed them to the girl.

I didn't really want to win, he said. Nor did I, she replied. See you at preschool next year. Yes, maybe we'll be in the same class.

When I'm older, I'm going to drive that fire engine for the parade, said the boy. That would be good, said the girl. Can I ride with you? Yes, that should be okay, said the boy. We can wind the windows down, and if we drive really fast, the air will rush through and we'll be cooler than everyone else on the street.

sissy

★ Westdale

Where the great wandoo forests abut open farmland, there's a sense of possibility that can corrupt as much as stimulate mystery. The edge effect has implications that police and locals are all too conscious of. Casual dope smokers get ideas into their heads, and think about the depths, the center, hiddenness and obscurity. Statistically, it's males who get busted growing dope plantations in the forest, but this is a story about the enchanted queen of plantations, Sissy of the dope world. From her small farmhouse on a rundown horse property of no more than a hundred acres, but snug against thousands of acres of state forest, Sissy sent her "boys" out into the ocean of scrub and ghostly trunks of white gums to plant, nurture, defend, and harvest premium heads of marijuana. A natural girl at heart, she eschewed the easier hydroponics bonanza for good old-fashioned outdoor dope. She sold it by the ounce, the pound, the kilo. She'd done it for years, and never looked like being caught. And when various crops and various boys fell to the law or to rivals, she came out smelling of roses.

Sissy recruited her followers—her "assistants"—in a variety of ways. First, by advertising for farmhands. Low pay, but free room and board. Second, by inviting strangers at the pub home for a "smoke" if they looked the type (and who'd say no? She wasn't a beauty, but was "unusual," "compelling," even "hot" and enticing). Third, by giving lifts to hitchhikers, especially backpackers from elsewhere in the world, out on the bush roads looking for casual work and adventure.

Raj met her while backpacking after finishing university. He was from Sydney, but had studied in India and Cambridge. Raj was on the eternal journey around Australia, and wanted to get "off the beaten track" as much as possible. He wanted a change—no, *changes*. Constant difference. He was sick of "the same." He knew he'd go back and become what everyone expected of him, but for the time being he was taking the chances, the "anythings that go." He told Sissy as much when she picked him up in her four-wheel drive.

She sussed him as a smoker straight away and threw him a deal bag full of Thai Buddha. She'd imported this one, paying for it with her homegrown. Roll a joint, she said, there are papers and tobacco in the glove box. You'll find a lighter there as well. Raj didn't need telling twice. He took liberties (which she liked to see) and rolled a "three papery." Phew, instant hit. It was a solid stone, but he could handle it.

Would you like to come by my place to meet the boys? They're from all around the world. Otherwise, I can drop you into town. Raj wondered about the "from all around the world," being as Australian as anyone, his parents' parents Sikhs from New South Wales. But he looked at Sissy out the corner of his eye, beguiled by her radiance, her sweetness of intent, her green, almost feline eyes. There's no prejudice in this flaxen-haired woman, he said to himself, she's just generalizing because I am a backpacker on the road. No worries, mate, he said. Then: Yeah, sure, that'd be great. I've got time on my side—it'd be great to see your place, he said, arcing up the joint, inhaling, then passing it over as etiquette compelled.

You're a sweetie, she said. What's your name? Raj, he replied, and with that the next leg of his journey was decided. He quietly congratulated himself on his good luck. It's a random world, he said, euphoric with dope and company.

Raj kept an eye out for any rival as soon as they left the bitumen and hit the gravel. A pair of old wagon wheels stood sentinels on each side of the open gate. Horses in poor condition dragged themselves around the paddock to the left, and the odd donkey chewed stubble in the paddock on the right. The vehicle crunching along the corrugated drive didn't deter or disturb them at all; they took no notice. Wagtails picked insects off their backs.

They don't look too well, Raj said. The driveway seemed inordinately long. He could see a work shed in the distance, but no sign of a house.

Rescue animals, Sissy said after a while, and gave a little laugh. I look after them where others would send them to the knackery. It's a reward for having lived a life.

The drive curved suddenly around a clutch of great pepper trees as they passed the shed, gleaming a sickly silver in the sun. Then suddenly they were in front of the house, tucked in a gentle fold in hills he'd not even registered before. Behind the house, the vastness of the forest. Gee, he said, you've got nature at your fingertips. That I have, Raj, that I have. Now grab your kit and come in and have a beer and a few bongs. He couldn't quite believe his luck.

Led Zeppelin's "Whole Lotta Love" was blaring as they entered. One of the boys is rocking out, she said. Retro, said Raj. The music was really loud. Raj's voice made a vibrato against the trembling air. It was like being on the diaphragm of a speaker. He could see decorative mugs shuddering on the kitchenette. Wow, full-on! he yelled. Pulling a chair out from the

table for Raj and motioning for him to sit, Sissy disappeared. A
few seconds later the music was turned down and she was back
in the room with a deal bag and a bong. She took a bowl from
the kitchenette, a pair of scissors from a drawer, and managed
to procure a couple of beers from the fridge as she passed,
closing the door with her heel. She moves with such grace,
thought Raj. This is so cool.

As he took a few swigs from his can, she mulled up. He was
bursting with questions. Where will I be sleeping? There was
an edge to this thought. She looked so fluid under those baggy
work clothes. Did any of the "boys" share her bed? When would
he see them? He felt like poking his nose into the other rooms,
just to look. Then he had a sudden urge to piss. But before he
could ask for the toilet, Sissy said, Toilet's down the corridor
to the left. She pointed ahead, in the opposite direction to the
doorway the music had come from.

Raj knew she could see him all the way. He went straight
to the toilet and pissed. Wash your hands in the bathroom—use
any towel. He pushed a door, found the sink and a towel. The
bathroom window was open—he looked out onto the forest.
There were a couple of people, a couple of creatures emerging,
carrying pots, sacks, and shovels. Their age was indeterminate.
They were male, but covered in vast amounts of unkempt hair
so it was hard to tell much else. Their clothes were rags and
they looked filthy, stooping, and with a loping gait.

Raj shuddered as they approached, though they clearly
couldn't see him, their eyes fixed on the ground. He half-
imagined they grunted. They turned right angles suddenly
and broke off in the direction of—well, the shed. That's where
the shed would be from their perspective. They didn't look
up, though, so perhaps they had no perspective. They were
following a well-worn path. Sissy called, You all right, Raj?
Billy time—smoke up!

He picked up the bong and a lighter, and pulled. He
coughed hard. He was a hardened smoker, but the weed's

strength caught him by surprise. Sorry, sorry. A bit harsh? asked Sissy. No, no, hacked Raj, it's mega-sweet, just really strong. And it hit him, full-on. He felt as if he were falling through a projector, a flap of black-and-white film fluttering against the lens, making a waterfall on the screen. Yes, Raj, my weed is the best. Once bitten, twice shy, my love; once bitten, twice shy.

It was exquisite there when the sun rose over the trees. Raj had learnt to embrace the ghosts of wandoo as they retreated deep into the heart of the forest with day's arrival, in the same way they drew him towards them when evening fell. He wasn't sure how long he'd been at Sissy's place, but he felt one with the land, with Sissy.

He had enjoyed the comforts of her bed for a few weeks, then moved into the shed with the other boys. He was okay with that, it seemed evolutionary. He followed the others out into the forest and planted and tended the marijuana crops. In a few months it would be harvest. Sissy said his job would be done after that, and he could retire to the farm and enjoy the fruits of his labor.

Raj no longer saw the old horses and donkeys filling the paddocks as sad and lonely and worn out. They were rescue animals given new life where no life had remained. No one asked anything of them. They were fed and watered and left to contemplate the eternal beauty of the place.

It had been a fine harvest. He no longer needed to smoke or eat the dope to enjoy the fruits of his labor. He was one with the cycle of growing. He no longer needed to look where he was going; he could smell his way. He knew the trails as if they were his veins. Coming out of the forest he happened, unusually, to look up and saw a handsome young man—yes, handsome—

looking at him through the bathroom window. You lucky bastard, he thought, you've got it all before you.

And then he smiled to himself, a strangled laugh from deep in his throat. He hoofed at the ground, and snorted the dank air. A wagtail worked at his hair. It's feeling a little matted, he thought. How long since he had washed almost crossed his mind, but it was lost with the effusions of the environment. Soon, *soon,* he would be grazing the paddocks. Soon even the last of his worries, the last of his yearnings, whatever they were, would be gone.

the life history
of a wheatbelt
music teacher

★ Quairading

When Miss Lutz came into money, she knew exactly
what to do with it.

The town of Q. lay just over an hour east of Northam and
was one of the state's important wheat places. Miss Lutz, as she
now called herself again, had married into an old family during
the fifties, and though she was "getting on," she felt she still had
the drive for a bold enterprise.

Miss Lutz was an item of the furniture now—part of the
town's history. But it hadn't been like that during her early
years there, when being married to the postmaster was no
passport to acceptance. In some ways this is surprising, because
the postmaster is a pillar of these wheatbelt towns, and her
postmaster came from one of the first "settler" families in
the district. But it was not only Europe and music Miss Lutz
brought with her to town. She brought some very odd views.

Miss Lutz, who had arrived in Fremantle on a ship from
London, was Jewish. Before the war, her mother had sent her
from Holland to London to stay with an aunt. She never saw

her mother again; nor her father, who was in Poland when
the Nazis invaded. The aunt looked after her, trained her as
a pianist—if not of concert standing, certainly more than
proficient—and, on dying, left her the small amount of money
she had. In London, Miss Lutz noticed a poster as she passed
Australia House and decided to take advantage of assisted
passage to Australia. She walked straight in, there and then, and
began the process. She had no idea why—or that's what she
always claimed.

She met Sam, who had just been made postmaster in the
town of Q., in Perth at a dance a year after her arrival. She
liked a dance, and the Embassy Ballroom was the place to be.
Ruby, whom she'd met on the boat coming out, had told her
about the dances. If you want to meet an eligible man, that's
the place. And you'll love the music. And she did. Miss Lutz
loved all music, and she liked the barn dance as much as the
waltz. She met lots of farmers' sons, lots of men with prospects.
She wasn't beautiful, but "interesting," and that was enough
for them to flock to her for dances. Miss Lutz wanted to be
married. She wanted stability. She wanted a family. But though
being "interesting" might bring attention on the dance floor,
it did not necessarily lead to marriage proposals. In fact, her
"gentle accent," her love of music, even in a place where music
played endlessly, seemed to count against her. One young man,
as he swirled her around, told her she *thought too much*. And she'd
barely said half a dozen words to him!

But after a number of months and many dances, Sam
invited her onto the floor, then asked her again and again.
Then the next week, and the week after. They didn't talk
a great deal, but they moved well together, and Miss Lutz
found Sam a well-organized and polite young man. I am
a farmer's son, he told her, but I am a third son. I will not
inherit the farm. But I have just taken over from my uncle as
the postmaster—the youngest postmaster ever in the district.
I have a house attached to the post office, and I am looking

for a wife. He was that forthright. Miss Lutz admired this a great deal.

Sam didn't want a big fuss. He wanted to marry quietly in Perth, in the registry, and take his bride back home after a few days in Bunbury on the coast. It was then that Miss Lutz told him she was Jewish. Sam had never asked anything about her beyond where she came from. She'd said London, which made him look oddly at her—no doubt because of the accent and the name—but he left it at that. I am not religious, Sam, but I am Jewish. He wasn't sure why she bothered to tell him that. To tell the truth, he wasn't even sure what "Jewish" meant. He did know the Bible said that the Jews were the chosen people, and that seemed fine by him. He asked if it was good being Jewish, and she said, yes, she thought so. She was proud of it. And that was the sum total of their conversation on the issue.

Miss Lutz loved her husband, and she loved her new home. She loved driving out in the old Ford around the district, to see the crops being sown and harvested. She loved the smell of freshly cut hay. She loved cooking for her husband.

But Miss Lutz was not loved by Sam's family, nor by most of those in the town. In fifty years she was never to be told why. No one ever said a negative word to her—they all smiled in passing, and the family always invited her to the special occasions and gatherings. At Christmas, they'd sometimes make uncomfortable remarks . . . but, on the whole, the simmering prejudices were held back.

What's more, the better of the town's citizens were pleased to have such a talented musician in their presence. She was not a schoolteacher, but the music teachers at the school—and many came and went over the years of her life in town— always sent their most talented prospects to Miss Lutz for honing or polishing or sharpening up. As a "private music teacher," Miss Lutz trained generations of daughters to read music, to play the piano, and to sing.

But the bugbear centered on church. There were three churches in that small town—Anglican, Catholic, and Baptist. All would have liked her to play the organ for them, but they couldn't bring themselves to ask. On occasion she played at her own suggestion, but she could see the holy men shrink under their collars, cassocks, and suits. It was as if perdition was just around the corner. She stopped offering early on.

In reality, her Jewishness, which Sam had mentioned to his family at first as an idle "fact," and which had become a talking point in town for the first few months she was there, became a forgotten fact. No one really knew anything about her origins or ethnicity beyond her being "European." Like Ferraris and Citroens, it all seemed a little exotic, and, to be honest, stuck up. It was that, they claimed, they distrusted, when all was said and done. And it wasn't because she didn't have their church or belief; it was that she seemed to have no belief other than music. When people went to the post office, as one has to, you'd hear her playing coming down through the post-office roof, as the lounge room was overhead, or you'd hear her record player singing out of the window into the main street. True, it was beautiful music. Beautiful. And she could teach as well as any lady down in the city. But was that enough?

Miss Lutz smiled through her life but after the first few years with her husband found that she really only loved her music. Oh, she loved the natural world, and she loved her husband well enough, but she loved them in the context of music written about such things. Music was the only protection from a devastating and crushing loneliness. She and Sam had never been able to have children. And she saw in the eyes of the ladies of town that this was further evidence of her oddness, of her Europeanness.

After Sam's death, Miss Lutz inherited a vast amount of money she didn't know he'd had. As his family had died, he had inherited chunks of land and sold them off, but said little or nothing to her. She was never privy to family business. He always gave her enough, and she never asked for more. It struck her now how strange it was, to have lived that way for so many years. She lived in darkness. Her music hid the fact that she was in a darkness she couldn't emerge from. Her music didn't take her from the darkness; it hid the darkness.

Miss Lutz was wealthy, and it meant nothing to her. She felt angry at the town when she realized how alone she truly was. So many people at her husband's funeral, and no one wished her well, or shared condolences. They just nodded or smiled slightly. She'd been cut loose from them now. She was even too old to teach music to their children. But she wasn't really too old; she knew that.

So Miss Lutz established a music scholarship at the District High School. It was to be called the Miss Lutz Scholarship for Music. She meant no offense by not using her husband's family name—which was, by the way, Brown . . . she had been known to all as Mrs. Sam Brown, the music teacher. The conditions of the scholarship were three months to be spent in a capital of Europe to learn of its music traditions and the significance of Jewish contribution to the musical culture they took for granted. On top of this, the scholarship would pay for a student to stay at one of the university colleges in the city and to study at the university, should their grades be adequate and they gain university entry, for three years. The award was to be offered every three years. With such a vast amount of money on offer, none of the Anglicans or Catholics or Baptists or other denominations could bring themselves to oppose it. Or, indeed, to refuse it, should it be offered to their child. And why would they? They were proud to be such an important center of the arts in the middle of the wheatbelt.

After fifty years and, *finally,* an historic part of the town, Miss Lutz settled down in the small house she had bought for herself not far from the post office where she had spent most of her life. Other than making the occasional journey to Perth, "the big smoke," to buy records or for a medical appointment, she had never really left the town. People smiled at her when she passed. She knew they were real smiles. She knew that, deep down. Though she was old, she still had one or two students who came to play the upright piano in her front room. Inevitably, these were students with their eye on the Lutz scholarship.

So Mrs. Lutz sat back in her lounge room and listened to Felix Mendelssohn's *Fingal's Cave*, at home where she was, but at the same time, a long way away.

the offering

★ Wagin

It was a long, hot walk from town to their new "making-a-go-of-it place" in the paddocks. She was angry because she'd trusted him. A small house, almost a shack, two pencil pines, and acre on acre of painfully long dry grass. More than a fire risk; they already had one foot in Inferno.

And no bloody car. He'd lost his license for DD, and she'd never had a license. Both were hanging for a drink, and had walked into town in the heat with thirty dollars on them, craving a cold beer, but knowing they had to get by until Thursday, and there was practically no food in the house.

Thirty dollars, they'd mused. Two bottles of sherry, bread, rice, oil, potatoes, and a cabbage. That was it. They jammed the brown-paper bags of sherry into the plastic bags alongside the food. They held a bag each.

After a few steps he stopped, and started rolling a smoke. He licked the paper, handed it to her, and rolled a second one for himself.

She didn't look him in the eye, not even when he lit hers, then his, with his Bic, studying it in the light to see if the gas would last. Fortunately, Dave had left them a packet of rollie tobacco and papers for a housewarming.

Gotta start home brewing, he'd said to her earlier, as they'd walked briskly, mostly silent, along the gravel, then on the bitumen into town, cars passing close and slowing down enough to make them feel uncomfortable. He was a big bloke but, well, wasted looking. She was "mousy," some said unkindly.

She spoke. Finally, she spoke.

Maybe the frost is thawing in this damned heat, he thought. Then he laughed to himself. About ice. He'd recently kicked the habit, and put them through hell. She looked at him like he was a gibbering idiot, and he shut up. He shut the fuck up, then wondered what she'd actually said. He hadn't really been listening. Usually she'd repeat it for him.

It's a shit of a walk. It's a shit of a house. It's a shit of a place. What had possessed him to drag them to a town that worshipped a giant concrete ram . . . ? Yes, that was it; much better. He hustled alongside her, trying to keep up.

And then disaster struck. The bag he was carrying—it had to be his—split, and the sherry bottle smashed to the ground. Medium-dry sherry flooded out through the torn brown paper bag.

That's yours, she shrieked. You're not getting any of my bottle!

He stared dumbstruck at the ground. The bread was about to fall through the same tear, and something moved his hand to catch it.

She kept walking as he fixated on the mess. With his sandshoe, he scraped it to the side of the path. Kids probably walk along here, he told himself. He looked around for a bin, then abandoned the thought, and the site of the disaster. Cabbage in one hand, bread in the other, he loped towards her, resisting the urge to look back over his shoulder. He'd have to be really sweet to her now if he was to get a swig of hers. She was like that. But then, so was he. They had rules. Their relationship survived through having rules. Especially when things were at their most stressed and difficult.

But as he was catching up, something strange happened. Maybe it wasn't quite an epiphany. But looking at her grubby skin-tight jeans, and that arse he almost worshipped, the determination of her stride in the scorching sun, both of them without hats, and bucketing sweat, he thought, No, no, I won't even try to cadge some of her bottle. I'll hang out. Tonight I'll make dinner. I'll make something out of the little we've got. From their last place, there were still some herbs and spices, including a packet of dried chilli. She loves chilli, he thought.

Beside her again, he said, Sorry, darl, really sorry. I'm not going to try and cadge from yours. She shot him a suspicious look—she knew him too well. He saw her clutch her bag closer. Don't worry, darl, I mean it. And I'll cook us a real nice meal tonight. Do me good to get off the grog for a couple of days.

She increased her pace. Possibly she was debating whether to cut her losses, hand him the bottle, and shoot through. Somewhere. Anywhere. Coming off the booze, he'd be a horror.

He meant every word, as far as he was able to mean anything. He'd convinced himself. After all, turning points start somewhere. And a sharp turn was better than a slow bend. The plunge. But then, she had no plans to stop. It'd be lonely. He relied on her company more than she relied on his. That caused him more anxiety.

He'd noticed it coming into town. A magnificent bottlebrush tree in full flower. Its brushes were glowing, making the heat seem tolerable. Even in their drooping, lilting laziness, the brushes were electric, full of life. They *chose* to laze because at any time they could spark in a way that didn't need to burn anything, didn't need to lead to conflagration, because they fueled themselves, were happy in what they were. He'd even walked close to the tree, going off the path, to let the red lashes stroke him, the pollen coat his arm.

She passed by the bottlebrush tree without a glance. He stopped, tucked the cabbage under his arm beside the bread, walked over to one of the most stunning blooms, and with his free hand snapped it off. He walked up behind her.

Ta dah! he said, passing his arm in front of her face so the his hand flourished the brush before her nose.

Quit clowning around, you jerk! she said. But once she got over the surprise, she laughed a little.

As she took the flower, her shopping bag slipped and burst. The potatoes and the remaining bottle crashed to the ground. They both stood still, frightened and tense, waiting for the off-blood pool of sherry to emerge, to vaporize in the heat, swirling addiction between their noses.

They grabbed each other's hands. Under one arm the cabbage remained firm; in his free hand he gripped the bread. They looked at each other laughing and crying. It was agony. It was too much.

They gathered up the potatoes, which she cradled in her shirt, placing the rice there as well. Then they started for home, their new home.

Wait, darl, he said. He went back and kicked the bottle off the side of the road. It was still intact in its brown paper bag. It was a tough bottle and had struck the ground in just the right way.

It was one less thing for them to carry in the heat. One less burden to share.

the legend of
the boat

★ Perth/Canning River

I am a legend in these parts. Hardly a day goes by without some schoolkid coming to the river's edge—on both sides—looking out into the dark waters, and uttering my name in hushed but excited tones. My story will live forever, and that's a great comfort to me. My kind of kid wants nothing more in life, I reckon.

It is not a great river, but the distance between opposite banks is substantial. And it is deep enough. Even partway out towards the middle, you can't dive and touch the bottom. And as you dive down trying, it gets murkier and a cold current hits you hard, as if the river has two layers with the bottom layer off-limits. And down in the cold place, down where the body heats up and your skin stings, it is silty and murky and you can't see your hand. It's a healthy river, though—plenty of kingfish and flathead and fleets of jellyfish. You get the brown speckled sort that hang in the water like weed, and the white flat discs that propel themselves against the currents, staying still or ending up marooned and dried out like frisbees along the shores. There's not much beach, but where there is, it glows white as bone. Mostly, it's reeds and paperbarks and banks that are steep.

For years I played down on one of the sandy shores, not far from our house. I was a good swimmer, and since I had grown up near the river, my parents never worried. When I was old enough, I started to swim out to an old concrete boat moored in the middle of the river. Well, not really the middle, as where I went was an inlet off the main part of the river. Still, it was as far across between banks as anywhere, and that old concrete boat, which was covered in shag and seagull poop, was in the middle, and that's a long way. I tried to reach it for years, but I wasn't strong enough, or a little too frightened, and always turned back. But when I was twelve, I reached it, and with that slightly panicky feeling of not being able to secure a grip and swallowing some of the dark water, I managed to pull myself up the mooring chain and clamber on board.

From the deck, I could see other kids across the river waving to me. I waved back, then explored the boat. The cabin was padlocked. I couldn't see anything through the narrow windows along the side of the cabin, as they were painted over with rough white brushstrokes, and through the spaces between the paint I could see thick curtains and nothing more. I'd always wondered how the boat got there and whose it was. I never saw anyone go out to it. Dad had said it was concrete, and I remember wondering how it could float. He told me. It was white and red. Though it was large and rose a long way out of the water, there wasn't much room on the decks. I sunned myself on top of the crusted and wet bird poop on the cabin roof. I needed to get my breath back and build up my strength before swimming back—it was a long, tiring haul, and I was at my limit in reaching it. I am not a stupid kid.

Heading back to the shore, I wanted to do a spectacular dive, but I knew I wasn't up to it. What's more, those other kids playing on the far shore wouldn't see it unless I dived off their side of the boat, and that would put more swimming in the way of getting home. And I really didn't want to make a big scene of it, since maybe the owner lived in one of the mansions across the road from the river's edge, and I'd cop it. So I just tin soldiered in on "my" side and swam slowly but steadily back to the shore. Crawling out of the water, I said to myself it'd be a long while before I tried that again.

A few weeks later, I was mucking about in the shallows, and I looked up to see two kids on top of the concrete boat waving to me. They were yelling as well, but I could only just hear them as the sea breeze was in and it was blowing the wrong way. I knew it was them—the kids I'd seen playing on the far shore. They were showing me they could do it as well! I waved back, and thought, okay, tomorrow . . . after school. It was getting too late to go there and back today.

We must have set off from our opposing shores at about the same time, because we met at the mooring chain. They were boys of my own age and build, and we all laughed when we grabbed the chain and grappled to get up, and fell in. Phew, it's a long way out, one of them ventured. And I, gasping a little, said, Yeah, you climb up first. And they did, and I followed. We all flaked out on the cabin deck and down near the tiller. Bit crampy, said one of them. Yeah. The breeze had picked up a little and the boat swung on its moorings. Boy, that feels weird, I said, as I felt like my stomach was being left behind. Our dad—it turned out they were brothers one year apart in age—reckons this boat's been a danger for years. He reckons it was built by an old bloke who died. And with that we kind of all twisted around from our resting places to gaze at the rusted padlock. Wonder what's in there? Yeah. But as it turned out, we were all good boys—too good—and left it at that. We probably all wanted to bust it open, but we had no way of doing it easily and didn't want to take more of a risk than we already had. We felt collectively brave. We yarned for ages, but though it was summer and the evenings long, we had to get back to our homes. We agreed to meet again on the boat in a few days, but a bit earlier. The long summer holidays were coming to an end, and it would get much harder for two of us during the year—dreaded high school was upon us.

They were already there when I clambered up the rope for our second meeting. It was an excellent day. Not too hot, just a gentle breeze with the boat sitting steady at its mooring. The other boys had brought out rags and were doing their best to wipe the poop away. They'd also brought a screwdriver, which was sitting on the cabin roof, glinting in the sun. How did you get that out here? I asked. Wrapped it up in the rags and shoved it down my boardies, said the older boy. The younger one said, Yeah, looked like he had a stiffy. We all laughed, though I was a little embarrassed, I have to say. Nearly slipped out about five times. They laughed again. Nah, wrapped it up and put it in the pocket of my boardies. These ones have big pockets, he said, turning the webbing out to show me. What's it for? I asked, full knowing. In answer, the older brother jammed the screwdriver in the cabin latch and hit it with his palm, snapping the brittle metal. Let's take a look! I wanted to dive off the boat, there and then, and head back. They were going to wreck a good thing. But I stayed.

Inside the cabin there was pretty well nothing. Gee, I thought we'd find the old bloke's body, the younger brother said. Seems like he never finished it, I said. There was a lot of water swishing around down the bottom. It was deep and dark like the river. In the half-light streaming in through the door, I could see an oily film on the sloshing water. It's like a tomb, I said. It gives me the creeps. Yeah. And we went up and shut the door and jiggled the latch back into place and banged the screws loosely back in with the handle of the screwdriver so we could at least imagine that whatever spirits lived in that dingy emptiness would stay in there. We didn't refer to it again, but found our sunning spots and talked about school and model planes and even girls a bit, though not much.

The afternoon passed and we started to get hungry. Why don't you swim to our side and we'll get something to eat? the younger brother suggested. Yeah, said the older one, we live a few houses back from the river. I was going to say that I lived on the other side and it was no further to go to my place, when I remembered Mum was having "the girls" around for afternoon tea, and that turning up with two new mates might be a bit awkward. And I was curious, so why not? There was plenty of time. And it'd be another first—the first kid at my school, I was pretty sure, and their school as well, to swim from one side of the river to the other. I wouldn't need to mention the boat in the middle when telling the story on my first day at high school. Kudos!

The brothers' place was much like mine. Their mother was much like mine. And their dad worked in the city as well. Their bedrooms looked like mine. Model planes dangled from the ceiling on fishing line, and the air stunk of Airfix glue. Gets you high, the older brother whispered, and winked. Then we played a game of wars using their Africa Korps and American toy soldiers, and the time ran away. Hey, I better get going, I said, after a couple of hours. Gee, yeah, they said. Do you mind if we stay here and finish the battle? the younger brother pleaded. Nah, no worries. See you on the boat next weekend? Yeah, maybe Sunday afternoon?

So I walked down to their shore. I thought how weird it'd be swimming to the boat from their side. A new experience. And looking across from their side to mine. I couldn't recall ever having been around there in the car with Mum and Dad. Maybe when I was too little to remember. I got to the shore and looked out, growing giddy and confused. My stomach went into my mouth. There was no boat. I couldn't be lost; it was only a few houses. Airfix glue. I was always paranoid about glue. No. It was the right place—I could see my beach, and knew the houses behind. Small from this distance, but still recognizable. The boat had vanished. Gone. Someone had taken it away. I searched the waterline for the red buoy that bobbed off the chain when the boat was moored. I thought I could see it, but the breeze had picked up and was blowing into my face and, to make matters worse, was making the water choppy. A brown foam-capped sludge. I should go back to the brothers' and ring my mum to come and get me. I should. But I won't. I can make it. I'll just tread water and hold on to the buoy. I'll be a legend. A real legend. I'll honestly be able to say: I swam the river, and without any help. No, I'll be able to say I swam there and back. The boat being there on the way over doesn't count, and there's no evidence to contradict me now. High school is going to be great! So I set out, swimming firmly into the chop.

The buoy wasn't there. Nothing was. Then it was there and I grabbed at it, but it sank only to bob back up as a kind of slow torture when I let go. I pushed away from it, then looked again, and there was nothing. I swallowed foam and algae and felt the jellyfish smothering me. I turned away from the breeze and could breathe better as I trod water. I could swim back to the brothers' shore. I could. Be like surfing in. But it would be shameful. Nothing like shame. It burns your ears. Legends don't feel shame. Or don't show their shame.

I turned towards home and changed my stroke to make it easier: breaststroke. Then as I wearied, I tried backstroke. Then sidestroke. But I got more and more tired and tired. I dived under the waves and swam holding my breath. It was easier. I surfaced, took another breath, and did it again. Somehow I had gone backwards. I seemed to be back at the spot where the boat had vanished. I knew it was the spot, I could feel it inside me. My nanna used to say, "I could feel it in my waters," and I knew what she meant. It amazed me how clearly I was thinking. Legends don't panic, and I wasn't panicking. If anything, time was slowing down to a really pleasant pace. I could hear the river. I could feel it inside me. And then I dived down again, and kept pushing myself down until I pierced the second layer, swam into the cold silt and as I went further I got so cold that I got hot, and then I reached out and touched the stern of the boat, and I opened my eyes and could see it as bright as day, shining white and red out of the gloom. I pulled myself along the railing down from the stern to the cabin and found the door wide open—the screws having come out as it went down. I pulled myself into the space which was light and well stocked as if for a long voyage down the river and into the ocean. There was a comfortable bed made up, and I lowered myself into it, breathing the crisp ocean air, already flooding the cabin. I would circumnavigate the world in this boat, this old concrete boat. I had been blessed. I would be a legend. I *am* a legend, as you know.